It's Always Something

Vol.14 of Indian Creek Anthology Series

© 2007 Southern Indiana Writers

It's Always Something
Volume 14 of the Indian Creek Anthology Series

Copyright © 2007 Southern Indiana Writers

Each selection herein © 2007 by the author or artist

ALL RIGHTS RESERVED

Published by Southern Indiana Writers, 2200 Reno Ave., New Albany, IN, 47150
Book designed by T. Lee Harris

ISSN 1085-357X
ISBN 978-0-6151-8495-1

Cover Art and design by T. Lee Harris

Contents

Home on the Range

by
Marian Allen

My life was so simple, before I got my heart's desire.

I had always wanted to live in the country. Nobody I knew lived there, but my elementary school readers were full of pictures of Dick and Jane and Sally and Spot and Puff wandering around unsupervised under a round yellow sun. According to them, carrots and spinach were good in the country. Since I had to eat the damned stuff anyway, it seemed natural to dream about living where veggies actually tasted like something edible.

Granny Babs, who watched me while Mom and Dad worked, had been through the Depression and World War II rationing. With me to help her, she had most of her big back yard put out in vegetables. Her property butted up to the Forestry, where she took me hunting for wild mushrooms, blackberries, fiddlehead ferns, watercress, and all that wilderness fodder.

The kids at school called me "Wilder", after Laura Ingalls Wilder of "Little House on the Prairie". It was certainly better than my given name—which was Mamie Jane Nael—and it even sounded cool, during my rebellious teens.

In my junior and senior years of high school, I worked at Cloverburg's Health Blossom Food Cooperative. I worked there during the summers while I was in college getting my Health and Nutrition degree ... and for seven years after that, when a Health and Nutrition degree didn't translate into any other job.

By that time, I had turned into a vegetarian. Not just a vegetarian, but a vegan, which is not an alien race from outer space, but a person who eats only plants—no meat, no eggs, no dairy. Granny Babs and Mom had taught me to cook, and the urge to convert the family to my diet drove me to construct vegan meals they couldn't resist.

That led to my first cookbook, VEGAN FOR MEAT-LOVERS, written under the name of M. J. Wilder. It had very respectable sales—for a vegan cookbook. The second, M. J. Wilder's VEGAN AND LOVING IT, did even better. The third, M. J. Wilder's MEATLESS

LOAF AGAIN?, was the best yet. I didn't make enough to retire on, but my needs were simple and I was single—I had a nice little umbrella for a rainy day.

Then Mom and Dad retired to Florida, Granny Babs passed away, her house burned to the ground, and an insurance check came addressed to me, her beneficiary. The day after I deposited the check, a customer came into Health Blossom—where I was *still* clerking—saying she and her husband were moving to California, and they needed to sell their place in the country—five acres on the other side of the Forestry from Granny Babs' old house. It would take me fifteen minutes to drive to work from there, less time than it took through traffic from my apartment.

Dream come true.

The house had been modernized, but didn't look it. There was a summer kitchen at the other end of a covered boardwalk, in good repair but in no way modernized, with a big old wood-burning cast-iron range for canning. Attached to the summer kitchen was a creekstone spring house, also in good repair. There was a barn, which the folks I bought the place from used as a garage, and there was a hen-house, which they had scrubbed and whitewashed and used to dry herbs. There was a rummaged-up area about half the size of a basketball court, surrounded by rabbit wire, that they called a garden, but was more like a place they tossed seeds and hoped for the best.

"We bought this place and fixed it up," my customer said, "and spent a month or so out here in the summers. We thought we might move to the country full-time, but we both work in the city and the commute would have been brutal in the winter, so the place has really hardly been used since we restored it. There's just one thing. There's a wild cow in the woods."

Her husband groaned. "You had to tell her that." He gave a little laugh. "It's some story everybody around there tells. About three years ago, one of the farmers lost a cow through a gap in his fence. He never found it. It was taken by a carnivore, if you ask me—a two-legged carnivore. But ever since then, there've been all these 'wild cow' sightings in the Forestry. Of course, nobody's seen it except for people who know the story, but that doesn't stop the legend, does it?"

"Everybody else thinks it's a deer," my customer said.

"What would it live on?" her husband wanted to know.

"There's lots of forage. Fresh stuff in the growing season and dry stuff in the winter. Plus, it could sneak into the farmyards and eat the tame animals' food."

He gave me one of those isn't-she-cute-when-she's-kooky looks, and I was really really glad I wasn't going to California with them.

"Well," she said, "just you be careful, that's all."

This was late winter. As the ground thawed and dried, I put the garden in order and planted early crops. I dug some beds around the house and outbuildings and planted edible flowers, which inspired a new cookbook: M. J. Wilder's TAKING THE NASTY OUT OF NASTURTIUMS. It made a big splash when it came out, but it didn't have staying power. After an initial burst of sales, it was remaindered. I could count on finding at least one copy in any book store bargain bin or library book sale I browsed.

Meanwhile, spring came, and I put on my rubber boots and long sleeves and went gathering in the woods. Every so often, I would hear the crackle of leaves and breaking twigs. A couple of times, I heard something heavy moving away in the distance, but thought nothing of it. It wasn't until the day when I suddenly thought, "Deer," that I remembered my customer's story about the wild cow.

After that, every time I heard a crack or thump, I snapped my head around toward the noise. Once, I was sure I saw a glimpse of black and white between two stands of trees, but it could have been the shadows of wind-blown branches.

I took to talking out loud. I took to stopping at the treeline before I went into the forest and shouting, "Just leave the mushrooms and a few fern tips, okay? There's plenty for both of us!"

M. J. Wilder's WILD AND WOODSY had a cult following with the historical re-enactment crowd, but didn't catch the interest of the general buying public. My other cookbooks were out of print and started turning up priced at under a dollar on eBay. I'm telling you, when the shipping is more than your book, you just want to shoot yourself.

Vegetarian titles were still selling, my publisher told me, but not vegan titles. If I could just slip an egg or some cheese into the

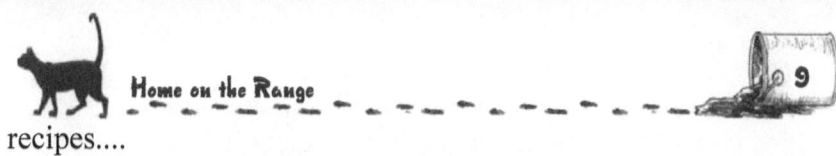

recipes....

Well, ick!—right?

Fortunately, I still had my day job. Only it was sometimes a night job. The store was open until nine, and then we had clean-up and, once a month, inventory and, twice a month, restocking. We rotated shifts and duties, so I didn't always work until midnight, but it sometimes happened.

Which brings me to that June night when I got home at nearly one, pulled into the drive, where I always parked my vintage VW, and saw a light in the summer kitchen.

I didn't think I had left it on—it had been broad daylight when I went to work. I remembered thinking, when I took the rhubarb pie out to cool, that it would have to wait until morning because I didn't want to come out to the summer kitchen to get it in the dark.

Still, there it was—on. Rhubarb pie sounded good, so I crossed the yard and opened the door.

As Granny Babs would have said, you could have knocked me over with a feather. I was simply too stunned to move.

You don't realize how big cows are until you find one sitting, totally uninvited, in your summer kitchen, tucking into a big slab of your rhubarb pie.

She didn't even have the grace to look ashamed. She froze when I opened the door, but then she met my gaze and deliberately took another bite of pie. Her big brown eyes were hard and challenging, and I had no doubt that this was the wild cow I had been warned about.

I knew I couldn't let her know how frightened I was.

"Is it good?" I said.

"Yeah," she said. "Be better with some ice cream."

She picked up a glass of white liquid and took a swig.

"...Is that what I think it is?"

"I don't know. Maybe you think it's wallpaper paste. But what it is, is milk."

"You drink *milk*?"

She smacked her lips. "Just like mother used to make."

"You drink *MILK*?"

"Hello? I'm a cow? What do you think little cows get big and strong from drinking—martinis?"

"I don't even want to *know* where you got it."

She snickered. "Actually, I bartered it from the dairy down the road."

"Bartered with what?"

She gave an evil grin and pantomimed taking a drag on a smoke—and I don't mean tobacco.

"Milk from contented cows," she said.

Well, there was just nothing to say to that.

"Don't stand there holding the door open," she said. "*You* weren't born in a barn. Come in. Sit down and take a load off. Have some pie."

"Nice of you to offer," I said, dryly.

She cut me a slice, put a fork on the plate, and slid it across the table.

"One piece of rhubarb pie," she said, "with a side order of sarcasm. You want some milk with that?"

"No, thank you."

"I wouldn't be so prissy, if I were you," she said. "Nothing wrong with lacto-vegetarianism, if you get your milk from an organic co-operative or something. Or a volunteer."

I must have looked as horrified as I felt.

"Wait till you're asked," she said. "I didn't mean me. Anyway, Mamie Jane—or should I say, 'M. J. Wilder'?—you really can't afford to keep writing these vegan books, can you, unless you just want to do it as a hobby? Your sales are in the tank—"

"How— What— You can't be reading my email!"

She smirked. "Hey, I'm homeless, not clueless. If you don't want anybody to hack into your wi-fi, you ought to put up a firewall."

With that, I picked up my plate. I nodded to the remains in the pie pan. "Take some and leave some," I said, and I meant it to sting. I went back to the house with her rumbling chuckle at my heels.

The next morning, I woke with the conviction that the summer kitchen incident had been a dream.

"I'll go out and bring the pie in," I told myself. "There won't be any pieces taken from it.... Except for the piece I obviously had on this dirty plate in the sink...."

But, when I went for the pie, I found only half of it—and a plate, fork and glass washed and left to drain.

I also found a note: "Nice meeting you. Thanks for the pie. Left you a little something in the cold room. Bossy."

Why the insult? I thought I had been more than hospitable, under the circumstances. Then I realized she wasn't calling me bossy; she had signed her name. Some things are so appropriate they go beyond irony.

The spring house was as cold as a refrigerator. At the beginning of my first growing season, it was also empty—except for the piece of paper on the floor, anchored by a chunk of rock. At the top, it said, in Bossy's bold scrawl, "I found some good stuff in the root cellar. Try this. You'll never go back." When I peeked into the spring, I saw the top of a ball jar. I reached in and fished it out. The liquid inside was pale yellow with buttery milk, and filled with chunks of potato and onion.

Of course, I wasn't about to eat it, but I couldn't bring myself to throw it out, either. My compromise was to take it to work. One of my co-workers, Helene, would eat anything.

She raved about it. Best potato soup she ever ate. She gave tastes to anybody else who didn't draw the line at dairy products, and they raved. They asked for my recipe. I said I was researching for another cookbook. They said to let them know when it came out, and they would buy it.

I drove home in a very pensive mood.

The first thing I did was go into the summer kitchen.

A casserole was on the table. Childhood memory suggested macaroni and cheese, but this wasn't the packet-of-orange-powder variety. This was real food, with broken-up sugar-snap peas and asparagus and baby spinach mixed in.

There was a note from Bossy: "I raided the garden. Sue me."

I left Bossy a note of thanks, but I couldn't eat the casserole, of course, on principle. I took it to work the next day. Again, it wowed the crowd.

As soon as I got out of the car at home, I could smell something heavenly. Bossy had struck again, with one of her nasty dairy foods. This had to stop. This was bordering on harassment. Wild cow or no

wild cow, I would just have to take my life in my hands and tell her to cease and desist. I threw open the door of the summer kitchen, determined to make my position uncompromisingly clear. But there, on the table, was a simmering fondue pot of wine-laced cheese and a plate of bread cubes. A note beside it said, "Eat till you bust. (ha ha) I'm playing pinochle with the girls tonight, so I grabbed a bite earlier. See ya 'round like a doughnut. Bossy."

I ate it. I did. I mean, if it didn't bother the cow, why should it bother me?

The next morning, Bossy knocked on the back door and handed in a plate of biscuits and milk gravy. What could I do but invite her in?

Over coffee, I said, "I'll admit, I'm surprised. I don't mean to be insulting, but I never would have expected a cow to be such a good cook."

"Why not? We're domesticated animals."

"...Yeah, I guess that makes sense. Listen, are you still living rough, out in the woods?"

She laughed. "I moved into the barn as soon as I realized you'd leave your car out in all winds and weathers rather than park it under roof and walk."

Well, wasn't she just Little Miss Hearty? "Oh," I said, rising above it. "Good. I mean, is that all right? Is the barn all right for you?"

She gave me a you're-so-weird look. "Of course the barn is all right. I'm a *cow*."

Enough was enough. I'm only human, after all.

"Yes," I said, pointedly. "I noticed. And I'm not sure I think it's such a good idea, you coming in and cooking and everything. I don't think it's sanitary."

There. I said it.

She put down her coffee cup and pushed it gently away.

"I see," she said. "Well."

She left. I didn't see her when I got into the car to drive to work.

At first, I rode high on a wave of self-righteousness. I had fallen from strict veganism, but I wouldn't have fallen if the cow hadn't tempted me. I was raised a Lutheran, though, so I kept running up

against the twin obstacles to self-righteousness: Bible-knowledge and guilt. To paraphrase Genesis 3, verse 13, "And the woman said, 'The cow beguiled me, and I did eat.'" It didn't cut any ice then, and it didn't cut any ice now. I was no longer a vegan. I had tasted Macaroni and Cheese Primavera and, as Bossy had predicted, I could never go back.

No, I couldn't blame Bossy. As the writer Damon Runyon said, "Never blame the booster for what the sucker does." Life is full of temptations. Most of us resist most of them. We can't blame the tempters when we fail, unless we want to give them the credit when we succeed.

Honestly, what had that cow ever done to me except offer me the best food she knew? And what had she ever asked for in return? I mean, other than whatever she could steal?

So I stopped by the farm supply store on the way home, and backed the car up to the barn door.

I knocked. I knocked again. And again.

Finally, a sulky voice rumbled, "What do you want?"

"I brought you something."

The double doors swung wide. Bossy's eyes were wary and red. I thought she may have been drinking, but I decided to let it slide.

"Look," I said, "I'm sorry. I was out of line. Way out of line."

"Not really," she said. "I guess maybe you were right. Who wants an old wild cow tromping around in their kitchen? Soon as it gets dark, I'll go back to the woods. That's where I belong."

"I'm asking you not to do that," I said. "I need you."

"Need me? Like you can't cook, or what?"

She was trapped in the most suspicious depths of her nature and experience. Kind words were not going to reach her. So I told her another part of the truth.

"Like you said, my cookbook sales are in the tank. I need a new angle. Lacto-vegetarianism might be just the thing. With your recipes and my experience in putting a cookbook together, we could be a hit. Naturally, I'd give you half credit—you could even have top billing—and we'd split the profits right down the middle."

"Yeah?" She was hooked. "Can I get that in writing?"

"Sure. Have your lawyer call my lawyer."

It was good to hear her laugh again.

I popped the car trunk and showed her my peace offering: A salt lick and a block of fancy alfalfa hay.

"*Now*," she said. "That's good eating!"

"And this." I reached into my pocket and pulled out a package of hairnets.

"Yeah," she said. "Yeah. Got to keep things sanitary, right?" She gave me a big brown-eyed wink.

MILKING IT FOR ALL IT'S WORTH by Wild and Wilder was a runaway sensation. We had to use our first profits to put a fence around the place to keep the reporters out. I was afraid Bossy might get a swelled head from all the attention, but her years on her own had taught her a healthy disregard for the opinion of the world, good or bad.

We planned a second book. Then, after another midnight restocking at Health Blossom, I pulled up and found Bossy waiting at the side of the house.

"We got trouble," she said, nodding toward the brightly lit summer kitchen.

I opened the door. The room was full of chickens, and the table was covered with a variety of quiches, still warm and fragrant.

One of the chickens slapped a wing on the table and leaned toward me, her black eyes glittering. She cocked her head and, with a hard smile, said, "Let's talk."

The Hair Says It All
by
J. Baumgartle

Hair brush obeys
upward strokes;
the whole mass stays,
an unexpected pose.
Face stares,
imagines situations
in which this self
might recur–
costumed perhaps,
for Halloween,
or laid out, for
some sci-fi culture's
burial rites,
or maybe it's
a low-grav moon-do.
More experiments,
face-covering
side-flopped
nose-crossing
ways to eliminate
future shocks,
encounter self
in all of its
appalling possibilities,
cope.

Caleb Speaks
By
Bonnie L. Abraham

Shalom. My name is Caleb. Daddy was Jephunnah – tribe of Judah. Guess you know all that though, since you've climbed all the way up here on my mountain. Good to meet you. Nice view up here, isn't it? Good breeze, too. But I suppose Jacob sent you to hear my story, not look at the view. I don't mind. It's kind of my mission. Maybe if you hear it often enough, you won't make the same mistakes.

I have to begin back at the beginning – in Egypt. You know that part of the story – you hear it every year at the Passover table. Moses came and told us God was going to free us from slavery. Then, for a while, it seemed like everything that happened made things worse instead of better. The Egyptians were undergoing the plagues God sent – and taking their anger and frustration out on us. We blamed Moses, and God, too.

But then the day came that Pharaoh said we could go and the Egyptians were so happy to see us leave, they loaded us down with their gold and jewels and best clothing. They couldn't wait to be rid of us – and the plagues.

We headed into the wilderness. Then Pharaoh changed his mind and came after us with his army. We were trapped between him and the Sea of Reeds. Moses held his staff out over the water and the waters parted. We walked – no, we ran as fast as we could – across on dry land with a great wall of water on each side. I don't know which was scarier – the walls of water or the army behind us.

By the time the last of us were across, Pharaoh and his army were right on our heels. But when we were safe, those walls of water just collapsed – and the whole army drowned. We were free – completely free of Egypt and Pharaoh and all of it.

That's when the grumbling began. Moses was the only one who had ever been out of Egypt before, and we were wandering around who-knew-where. We went three days without water, then found some at a place we named Marah. We called it that because the water was bitter – undrinkable. I don't know which was worse, being without water or having water we couldn't drink! The people were ready to revolt and go back to Egypt!

Moses prayed to God, and God showed him some wood. Moses threw the wood into the water and the water became sweet – drinkable!

From there, we went on to Elim, where there was plenty of water. Everyone was happy and we stayed a while, but then Moses said we needed to move on. We headed into the Desert of Sin, on our way to Mount Sinai.

I had been keeping a record, so I know it was on the fifteenth day of the second month after leaving Egypt when more trouble broke out. We were really low on food, and the people were grumbling again. They demanded Moses take us back to Egypt. But, once again, God provided. That's when the manna began. Every morning. And in the evening there was quail. But there were some rules: only gather enough for the day; don't try to hoard it for tomorrow. But what we gathered on the day before Sabbath was to be kept because there would be no manna to gather on the Sabbath.

Now, by that time, you'd think the people would have learned that God meant what He said, but no. There were those who tried to keep some for the next day. They ended up with a stinking mess full of maggots. The day before Sabbath, some of the people obeyed and gathered enough for two days. Those who had tried that before went and complained to Moses, but he reminded them of what God had said. Come the Sabbath, that same group went out to gather manna. They didn't find any, and God was angry and rebuked Moses.

Over and over, the people got into trouble and complained and God provided for them. He even saved them when they were attacked by the Amalekites. Joshua will tell you – it wasn't his skills as a military leader that brought victory.

At Sinai, Moses went up onto the mountain and God gave him the commandments. He brought them back to the people and we all agreed to obey them. But then Moses went back up the mountain, and the people grew impatient when he didn't come back down right away. In spite of the promise they had made to God to worship Him only, they built an idol and worshiped *it*. God sent a terrible punishment, but the people never seemed to learn. More than once, God threatened

to leave us on our own, but Moses interceded and God brought us to our destination.

There we were, in the wilderness of Paran, all primed and ready to enter the Promised Land. God had led us all the way across the desert from Egypt and we still remembered the plagues and the Sea of Reeds and how the Lord defeated Pharaoh's army. We had seen how God continually provided us with food and water, and how he protected us from the attack of the Amalekites. We knew God would do *all* He said he would do. At least, I thought we did.

Anyway, we were camped there at the edge of the Promised Land. Moses called us together and picked a man from each tribe. I was chosen for Judah, and my friend Joshua represented Ephraim. All the tribes were represented – except Levi, of course. They were priests.

Our orders were to spy out the whole land. Moses wanted to know everything: the lay of the land, city fortifications, the people, the crops. He even told us to bring back some of the fruit.

We traveled the whole land and brought back figs and pomegranates and grapes – why, one bunch of grapes from Eshcol was so big it took two men to carry it. It was truly a rich land God was giving us. After coming across the desert from Egypt, it was a sight to behold!

When we returned to camp, Joshua and I were all for going in and taking the land, just as God said. But the other ten? Scared out of their wits. And *they* scared everyone else.

You'd think they hadn't seen the Lord drown Pharaoh's army. Scared of a few giants! Hrummp! I tried to tell them. So did Joshua and Moses. But they wouldn't listen. They decided not to go in and take the land. They said it would have been better to have died back there in Egypt. Imagine!

Well, as a result, God told Moses he was going to wipe them out with a plague and start over! He would have too, only once again, Moses pleaded with Him not to. The other ten spies died there on the spot, but everybody else was ordered back out into the desert. Moses said we would leave the next morning.

Now you'd think the people would have learned their lesson, right? Nope. That next morning, they headed into the Promised Land! Naturally, they got creamed. They *still* weren't doing what God said.

We wandered around out there in the wilderness until Joshua and I were the only ones left of our generation. That was God's promise, you see – that Joshua and I would receive our portions of the Promised Land in spite of their unfaithfulness.

Well, I was 85 by then, but I could still fight. So I told Joshua to give me this mountain. It was full of giants, but God gave me the strength to drive them out and settle the land. God *always* does what He promises.

Sunday In The Park With Josh
by T. Lee Harris

Josh Katzen rolled toward the trilling cellphone, launching cats in all directions. Whozits and Boudicca dived off the foot of the futon bed and disappeared down the stairs. Flash, the largest of the three, bounced off Josh's bare shoulders to hit the bedside table at a run, scattering the contents like shrapnel.

Finding the cell was easy; it hit him in the ear. Finding his glasses was easy, too. He heard them crunch as he sat up to open the cell. He swore and peered at the ID screen. Dr. Avi Rosenberg – but Avi was in St. Louis at an archaeological conference making a presentation of a new data storage and correlation software.

Frowning, he answered, "Hey, Avi. What's up?"

Avi sounded tired. "Morning, Josh. Sorry for the early call, but we're in a bit of a bind and I told Connor you could help."

"Uh oh. What's happened?" He dug the remains of his glasses out and squinted at the damage. He was lucky. The screw holding the left lens in place had popped out. Fixable.

"Connor's in the hospital here in St. Louis. Another infection – real bad one and the docs want to keep him here for a while."

That got his undivided attention. Dr. Connor McCrae was a senior professor of computer science at the University of Chicago and the author of the software Avi was presenting at the conference. More than that, he was the stereotypical absent-minded professor; not a good thing for a severe diabetic. Friends worried Connor wasn't taking care of himself. Looked like they were right. "Oh geez. What can I do?"

"Here, let me put Connor on, then I'll split. From the sound of it so far, this is Need-To-Know, and I don't."

Ah, Katzen thought. *It's that kind of bind.* He really believed he'd left all that behind when Johsua Katzen came into being. Still, he couldn't complain. If his old life gave him a way to help the important people in this new one, all the better. He'd never refuse to help McCrae, and he certainly couldn't refuse Rosenberg. If it hadn't been for Avi's help, his new life wouldn't have been possible.

The sounds of the phone being fumbled brought him back to

the business at hand, then Connor came on. "Hello, Josh. Actually, it's just me that's in the bind. I'll understand if you can't help."

"Nonsense, Connor. You know I'll help in any way I can."

McCrae hemmed and hummed for a few before stating, "You probably know I'm a pretty good programmer."

Pretty good? Connor McCrae was one of the best. Katzen laughed. "I've heard rumors to that effect."

"So have other people, apparently." McCrae lowered his voice. "I've been working on a secret project for the government – *our* government. See, it's this analytical program and the one they had — "

"*Connor!*" Josh cut him off sharply. "Avi is right, this sounds Need-To-Know and I doubt I need to. What exactly is the problem?"

"Yes, yes, you're right. The problem is that I finished the program, but then I lost it and the gentlemen are coming to pick it up tomorrow. I'd planned to look for it when I got home tonight, but...." He trailed off into a sigh.

"But that's in the crapper," Josh finished for him. "How did you lose it, exactly? A system crash? I'm okay at recovering data, but this sounds too big for my skills."

"No, the system didn't crash. I saved the program onto a flash drive and I lost *that*. It must have fallen off the table."

"Could it have been nicked?"

"No. I'm sure it's there in the trailer. It probably just got buried." Katzen mouthed the word *buried?*

National security notwithstanding, his first stop was the optometry store to get his glasses repaired. This was in no small part because he was frustrated enough to stomp the things into the floor and be done with it. He'd wasted an hour trying to fix them himself, a masochistic session that ended as the frames finally sprang open and fired the tiny brass screw across the room. It had sailed unerringly for the floor vent and dropped neatly into it with a barely audible *plink*. Good thing he normally wore contacts. Still, he liked having the glasses as back-up.

A doughy young girl was working alone in the back of the store when he came in. She shot him a deer-in-the-headlights look and stayed planted in her chair. He looked pitiful and held up the baggie

with the frames and lens in it. "I had a disaster this morning. The screw popped out of the frame and got lost."

She grudgingly came around to the counter where he could read her name tag: Jennifer Ask Me, I Can Help. Taking the bag, she looked the contents over, then brightened a bit. "You'll need a new screw, then. Easy peasy!"

Jennifer disappeared into the back room where Katzen could hear the sound of her rummaging. And rummaging. And rummaging some more. His feeling of doom solidified when she started casting furtive glances at him around the doorframe. He sighed and settled into a chair.

When she emerged at last, he was heartened to see the lens secure in its proper place. He quirked a smile. "Did they defy you, too? I fought with them for an hour before they finally shot the screw into orbit."

"Ummm. Not exactly." His smile faded as she handed the glasses back, adding, "We were out of this type of screw so I had to use another kind."

Josh looked down. A shiny silver screw rose over the matte bronze frames by a good quarter inch. He looked up in amazement. "This is a bit large, isn't it?"

"I put a nut on it so it wouldn't come out."

"This looks like an antenna."

"Ummmm. There's no charge on that."

"Good."

He folded the satellite-ready eyewear into a case and stowed it in his jacket pocket. No help for it, he'd have it corrected later. Right now, he needed to get to the trailer park and find Connor's flash drive.

A half-hour later, Katzen pulled his ancient black RX-7 into the drive of the trailer park, called simply "The Park". He'd passed the faded home-painted sign with its grade school triangle pine trees and washed-out arrow twice before he finally noticed it set back from the road. Finding the trailer of Sammie Longbaugh, the elderly neighbor lady entrusted with the key, was cake after that.

Connor had given the number of her trailer (six) and added that she had a lot of stuff on her porch. The man had the gift of

understatement. Sammie Longbaugh's trailer bristled with kitsch. It whirled, tinkled, sparkled and flapped in the late morning breeze. Gnomes, kittens, bears and bunnies lined the steps onto the wooden porch whose gingerbread decorations and scroll-work plant hangers had surely been the death of a platoon of plunge-routers. He stopped, open-mouthed at the display, until a pair of gleaming gold eyes amid the folderol caught his attention. A sleek gray cat hunkered near an opalescent pink bowl of kibble, intently watching, ready to bolt, but reluctant to leave the food. A smaller black cat peered warily over the gray's back.

He smiled and crouched down, calling to them softly. After a moment, they sauntered closer and deigned to let him pet them. The trailer door opened a crack and a woman's voice warned, "Don't you hurt them."

Still smiling, he stood. "Don't worry, ma'am. I like cats; I have three of my own."

The woman stepped all the way onto the porch and regarded him with open suspicion. She was small and bird-like – in the same sense that a sparrow hawk is small and bird-like. Josh stepped forward, hand extended, deftly sidestepping the cats winding around his legs. "Hi, you must be Mrs. Longbaugh. I'm Josh Katzen, a friend of Connor McCrae's. I think he called you about –"

Her entire demeanor changed. "OH! Connor! Do you know where he's been? I pick up his mail for him every morning and he hasn't been over to get it for DAYS!"

Katzen paused, nonplussed. "Uhhhh. Yes, ma'am, he's in St. Louis – didn't he call to tell you I was stopping by to borrow his door key?"

The little lady suddenly looked very uncertain. "Call me? No, I don't think he's called me." She thought about it again, then asserted. "No, he never called me. I'm sure I'd remember that."

Realization dawned. He'd seen memory lapses like this before. Unless he was mistaken, the lady was in the early stages of Alzheimer's. He *hoped* he was mistaken. She seemed to be a plucky, likable person. It would be a shame for her to descend into that grey fog. He nodded. "I'm sure he'll call later, then. Anyway, he asked me to borrow his door key from you so I could get something from his trailer that he needs." He felt a nudge at his knee and looked down. The little black cat was patting at him in hopes of more ear scratches. He obliged it.

"Those are strays. I feed 'em so they stay close and keep the mice away."

"Sounds like a good idea to me. If I could get Connor's key, I'll just pick up his stuff and get it back to you."

"Oh, I don't have a key to his trailer."

"Funny, he told me you did."

"No, I have the key to his mailbox, though. I get his mail every morning, but he hasn't been home. Do you know when he'll be back?"

News of the infection and hospitalization were on the tip of his tongue, but he bit it back. There was no reason to alarm her just yet. Besides, he couldn't be sure she'd remember it if he told her. Instead, he said, "Connor and Avi Rosenberg will be in St. Louis for a while yet. There's a conference there."

"Dr. Rosenberg! I've heard Connor talk about him. Do you work at the university, too?"

"No ma'am. I'm an artist. I work with Dr. Rosenberg on archaeological digs." He sighed inwardly. This was getting him nowhere. Reaching a decision, he stepped toward the car. "Well, thanks, Mrs. Longbough. I'd better get moving."

She looked disappointed that she was losing her company. She called. "'Bye ... uh ... Kevin. You be sure to tell Connor to come pick up his mail."

"Sure thing, Mrs. Longbaugh."

He drove up two lots to McCrae's trailer and parked the Mazda in front of an extended cab pickup truck with a camper on back. Assuring no one was watching, he slipped his hand under the seat and withdrew a slim leather case that slid unobtrusively into his jacket pocket. Grumbling how it was a damned good thing he didn't *need* a key, he stomped up the overgrown walkway. If this went sour, Avi Rosenberg was gonna pay for it big time. His grumbling turned to a grin when got his first good look at the lock. One of the cheapest, flimsiest cylinders made. He could almost open the thing by breathing on it hard. He chose a metal pick from the case and had the door open before he completed the thought that he needed to point Connor to a better make of lock. Still grinning, he stepped in.

The grin abruptly disappeared as he surveyed the wreckage around

him. At first, he thought someone had been here before him and ransacked the place, then he remembered the infamous mess in Connor's office – but this was ten times worse. Maybe thirty. Suddenly, the word "buried" took on a chilling new meaning. He stepped over a toppled stack of computer magazines, closed the door behind him, and flipped his cell open, then hit speed dial #2. It rang once on the other end.

"Hey, Josh! Where are you?"

"Avi Rosenberg, I hate you."

"Ah, you're at Connor's place."

"Your mitzvah level will never recover from this thing you've done."

"Oh, come on, Josh. Do you see any sign of the thumb drive? He said it might be in the vicinity of the couch."

"I'll be lucky to find the couch."

"It can't be that bad."

Katzen's answer was silence.

After a moment, Rosenberg commented, "Well, we knew he wasn't a neatnik."

Josh managed an exasperated growl, but his incipient tirade was derailed by a knock at the door. "Oops, someone's here. I gotta go – but you *owe* me, man."

Folding the phone, he opened the door to Sammie Longbaugh on the rickety steel steps. She held a bulging plastic bag of envelopes. "Kevin! I'm so glad you're still here. Can you see that Connor gets his – *oh my land!*"

Sammie's eyes went wide as she looked beyond Josh to the mess that was Connor McCrae's home. He guessed that she, like Connor's other friends, hadn't seen the inside of the trailer before. Wordlessly, she stepped past him. Finally she managed, "But you can't even see the floor."

"Well, we knew he wasn't a neatnik," came out before he could stop it.

"Oh. My," Sammie said again, then suddenly remembered the bag she clutched against her. "I brought Connor's mail so you could give it to him."

He took the bundle. "Sure, Mrs. Longbaugh, I'll see he gets it."

"Call me Sammie. My name's really Lucille, but everybody calls me Sammie."

Deeming it futile to get Kevin changed to Josh, he said, "Sure, Sammie. I'll be sure he gets this ASAP."

She cast another dismayed look around the ruin. "Oh, Kevin, what are you going to *do*?"

Josh followed her gaze, then voiced the reluctant conclusion, "Guess I'll just have to clean it up." *Now if I could only find a conveniently divertable river....*

Two hours and twenty-one trash bags later, the flash drive still hadn't materialized. The carpet, however, was visible – in places, anyway. He'd managed to locate the couch, too. Straightening, he stretched his back and groaned. Progress was being made – he had to keep reminding himself of that.

There *had* been a couple of bad moments. Like when he opened the oven to put a stack of plates out of the way only to find a skillet with a mound of insulation bits resembling nothing so much as an old Jiffy-Pop popcorn pan. It didn't contain popcorn, though. When he'd taken tentative hold of the handle to pull it out, mice of all sizes sprang out and ran in all directions.

Then there was the possum in the bathroom.... It had taken a while to focus after that one.

His turtleneck and jeans were coated with cobwebs, too, turning black into mottled gray. Oh well. He'd have at it with the tape roller from the car later. Snatching up trash bag twenty-two, he flung it out the now-open front door toward the impressive heap forming on the patio. As it smacked into the pile, he heard a startled "EEEEP!" from just outside.

He peeked around the door to find a thin woman with dark red hair and a faceful of freckles, that declared the color genuine, staring at the recently landed bag. The tiny white dog she cradled spotted Katzen and launched into a frenzy of barking.

Josh came out onto the folding steel stair. "Oops! I didn't know anyone was out here. It didn't hit you, did it?"

Her eyes slid from the bag to Josh. She paused, then laughed. "Nope, but it sure did spook me. I all but squished Bear, here." She bounced the little dog, who let out a yap that drove needles through Katzen's eardrums.

He stepped down, hand extended. "Hi, I'm Josh Katzen, a friend of Connor McCrae's."

The woman freed a hand from her canine armload. "I'm Tina Kirkpatrick, I live next door in number seven. I could tell from the way Bear was barkin' and bouncin' there was someone over here and I *thought* Connor was away at a conference or somethin'."

Josh eyed the quivering animal. "Some kind of watchdog. Yeah, Connor was at an archaeological conference in St. Louis with Dr. Rosenberg, but I got a call from them this morning. Connor developed another infection in his foot and they slapped him in the hospital."

She gasped. "In St. Louis?"

"Yep. The docs want to keep him there for a bit, so Connor asked me to come by and pick up a few things."

She poked the pile of bags with her toe. "And clean up a little looks like."

"That was incidental." He grinned broadly. "I couldn't find what I needed to find without cleaning up. So I am."

Tina looked puzzled. "I ain't never seen the inside of his place. Is he messy?"

"You could say that. I hadn't been in it until today, either." He stepped back and let her climb up to peek in.

"Holy moley!" She looked back at him round-eyed. "It's no wonder he's sick so much."

Before he could answer, he heard a shout from behind him. "Heya, Tina! What's happening to Dr. McCrae's trailer?"

He turned toward the voice and saw a sturdy woman with two cocker spaniels on reel-leads coming toward them.

"This here's Josh, Rita. He's Connor's friend and he's helpin' out while Connor's sick in the hospital," Tina shouted back over his head.

"Connor's sick?"

An older man who reminded Katzen strongly of Chuck Yaeger was getting out of a car across the street, and stopped. "McCrae's down sick again? When'd this happen?"

Tina and Rita waved the older man over. Tina called, "Heya, Del! This here's Josh, he's a friend of Connor's."

Del shook Josh's hand gravely. "Del Barber."

"Josh Katzen."

"Glad to meet you, Katzen. What's happened to McCrae?"

"Another infection. A real bad one this time, I'm afraid. He took sick while he was in St. Louis with Dr. Avi Rosenberg and they have him in the hospital there." Josh cringed inwardly at the broken record of the statement, but there was no help for it.

Barber shook his head and Rita clucked in sympathy. Tina bounced Bear in her arms again eliciting another ear-piercing yip. Everyone flinched, but seemed used to it. "It's no wonder, neither! I never saw the like of the mess his place is in."

"Yoo-hoooooo! Keeeevin!"

Katzen sighed.

Barber asked, "Who's Kevin?"

Rita glanced down the way. "Oh. Sammie."

There was a collective understanding nod as the little woman hurried up with a plate and a steaming mug. She paused uncertainly when she saw the crowd. Josh called, "Hey, Sammie, join the kaffeklastch – and looks like you brought the coffee."

"Afternoon, Sammie," Del intoned with a lop-sided smile. "Don't look like you brought enough to go around, though."

She sniffed. "I brought this for Kevin. He's been working himself to a frazzle all day. I made cornbread, too." She pushed the plate and mug at Josh. "I didn't know how you took your coffee, so I didn't put any milk or sugar in it."

"That's fine. That's the way I take it, anyway."

Del leaned in and murmured, "Don't mind her, son. She's known me for twenty years and she still forgets my name from time to time."

More neighbors gravitated toward the impromptu gathering until it took on aspects of the Marx Brothers' infamous stateroom scene from *A Night At the Opera*. He chuckled to himself, sipped the coffee and listened to the neighborly chatter. He was starting to understand why it never occurred to Connor to move away. These were good people.

Trouble was, he really needed to get back to looking for the flash drive and there was no way with all these people here. Several were even sitting on the steps. He couldn't get back inside if he wanted to. He shrugged to himself. It didn't really matter. It was early yet, and truth to tell, he was

enjoying the company. He suddenly noticed Sammie at his elbow. She looked worried. "Hey, Sammie, what's up?"

She glanced around and whispered, "Oh, Kevin. I don't know what to do. I looked for Connor's mail and I seem to have misplaced it."

Not good. She didn't remember bringing it down earlier. He leaned in and reassured her, "Don't worry. I have it and it's safe. I'll be sure Connor gets it."

She brightened. "You will? Oh, good!" Then she gasped. "I better get back, I think I left the coffeepot on." Josh watched her bustle back to her festively decorated home and wondered if he could swing getting her a coffeepot with an automatic shut-off.

"That was nice. Most folks don't cut her much slack."

Tina was standing a few feet away, looking thoughtful. Bear was bounding around her legs, his entire body wagging.

"I don't see why not. It's probably hard enough for her without people giving her grief on top of it. She's a good friend of Connor's, too, that counts for a lot."

She treated him to a wide smile. "Seems to me Connor McCrae's lucky in his friends."

He stood back from what he was coming to think of as the Great Wall of Books, dusted his hands and made a mental note: *Holiday gift for Connor, one nice folding bookshelf.* Scanning the room, he nodded approval. It still looked like someone had lobbed a frag grenade into it, but order was being restored.

The couch became a palpable presence. Connor had stressed the device had last been seen in that vicinity. It hadn't turned up in the surrounding area, so that left under. Considering some of the questionable items he'd encountered so far, Katzen wasn't looking forward to sticking his hand under it. Too bad. That's why he was there in the first place.

Pushing back his sleeve, he flattened on the floor and reached in, grabbing the first wad of computer print-outs – just as someone banged on the open steel door. He yipped and came up fast, cracking his head on the metal couch frame.

As he sat up, rubbing his head and spitting his pony tail out of

his mouth, he saw Tina standing just inside with her hand over her mouth in a futile effort to smother laughter. He treated her to a rueful grin. "Okay, we're even. I spooked you, now you spooked me."

"I brung my boyfriend, Bud, over." She giggled and motioned to someone still outside. "Bud, this here's Josh. Now, I'll leave you boys to it, I got dinner on the stove."

Bud was built like a fireplug and his voice was a cross between a gravel crusher and a foghorn. "Quite a stack of trash ya got there, Katzen," he boomed.

Josh shrugged. "And just the start, I'm afraid. Connor is a bit of a pack rat."

"Gonna be the devil to move that outta here in that upholstered roller skate of yours. I can haul it off in my truck if ya want."

"That'd be great! I was going to ask where a good place to dump it was."

Bud flapped a beefy paw. "That ain't no problem. I do maintenance at a bunch o' places. They all got big dumpsters. I'll need a hand loadin' the pick'em-up, though."

"That's no problem, either. I'm glad to do it and greatly appreciate it!"

Bud headed down the stair and chuckled, "I consider it a favor to McCrae, he's sure done enough for Tina an' me."

It took longer than he expected to clear the pile-o-bags and the day was rapidly fading when he finally watched Bud's laden truck tool down the street. He turned back to the trailer and was suddenly very tired. With all he'd accomplished, he *still* hadn't achieved what he was actually there for.

He went right to the couch this time, no more detours allowed. Flattening on the worn seventies vintage shag again, he resumed digging with resolve.

Thirty minutes later, he'd almost filled another bag, and fear that he'd sent the trash off too soon was niggling at the back of his head, when he caught a blue glimmer under a pile of destroyed magazines. Holding his breath, he reached for it and his fingers closed on a hard object that felt right. He wasn't going to cheer yet. After all the false alarms that proved to be translucent drinking straws, plastic spoons and bits of soda cups, he was

wary. He slowly opened his hand and nearly let out a whoop. There it was, a sapphire blue, one gig USB drive with a translucent case and end cap.

Relief flooded over him like a warm wave. He sagged against the couch for a moment, just staring at the thing, then realized he needed to stash it somewhere. After a moment's thought, he pulled his silver neckchain up through the turtleneck of his begrunged sweater, slid the flash drive onto it, refastened it and slid it back down. Perfect. It flattened out imperceptibly against his chest right next to his Bastet amulet.

He heard footsteps outside and Tina's voice called, "Josh, you ain't under the couch again, are you?"

He came around to the door, laughing. "Nope. You don't get me that way twice."

She stepped in holding a thermos and a plate covered with foil. "Sammie's lights might not go all the way to the top no more, but she's right in that you been workin' all day and ain't ate much. I brung you some dinner."

"Thank you, you didn't need to go to that trouble."

"I was fixin' for me an' Bud. Wasn't no trouble to fix for you, too." She waved happily and bounced down the stair into the gathering dusk.

The night was beautiful out here. The city-glow of Chicago was still there, but was enough removed, you could actually see the stars. Katzen leaned against the weather-beaten bench that sat along the side of the trailer. He hadn't realized how hungry he was until he'd taken his first bite of Tina's rich stew. He sipped at the coffee from the thermos cup. She made pretty good coffee, too.

Resting his head against the aluminum siding, he closed his eyes and listened to the night noises. In the distance he could hear country music playing, people laughing together – and someone coming through the cornfield that abutted the trailer park. He was suddenly alert and off the bench, moving quietly in the direction of the sounds. It was probably kids. He'd seen packs of them in the park all day. As he moved closer to the crunching cornstalks, low voices reached his ears, whispering in – *Russian*? Okay. Definitely not kids.

"Will you quit grumbling? I tell you it will be simple!"

"That is what I am afraid of, Misha. It is never as simple as you

say it will be."

"He is at a conference that ends tonight. Besides, the good professor's dossier says he is chronically late. You have no faith, Vassi."

"Of course not. I was raised in a faithless society."

"Always the jokes. With such jokes one would expect you to have a better attitude."

"I dunno," Josh said in English. "Stomping around empty cornfields and soggy drainage ditches tends to make me cranky, too."

There was a sudden silence as the two dark shapes halted in their steps and strained to make him out in the dim moonlight.

Suddenly, Vasily Koulikov grunted in justification, then announced in English, "Ah. Joshua Katzen. You see? I said as soon as I saw his name as an associate, this was a bad idea."

"What are you guys doing here? I thought you were in a Peruvian slammer."

Vasily answered, "Sometimes the security is more relaxed than others."

"Bribed, 'em, huh?"

Mikhail Bukharin growled, "Comedians, I have no time for your banter. Katzen, we know who and what you are."

"Of course you do: Joshua Aaron Katzen, up and coming archaeological artist. Signed and numbered prints are for sale on my website www.joshkatzen.com. Original artwork is pricier, naturally."

Bukharin spat in disgust. Then, jabbing a finger into Katzen's chest uncomfortably close to the flashdrive, accused, "I am tired of prevarications. You are a thief. You are obviously here for the same thing we are."

"You're here to help me clean up my friend's trailer. Cool! I could use a hand, it's really a mess."

Over Bukharin's impatient snarl, he added, "Look, guys, beat it, okay? I really am cleaning Connor's place and I don't need more stress right now."

Through the exchange with Bukharin, he'd been watching Koulikov carefully. Mikhail Sergeiovich Bukharin was more prone to blowing off. If he moved, he'd telegraph it to the world. Vasily Yurikovich Koulikov was where the real danger was. He acted the clown, but he was the larger of the two, and as Katzen learned to his

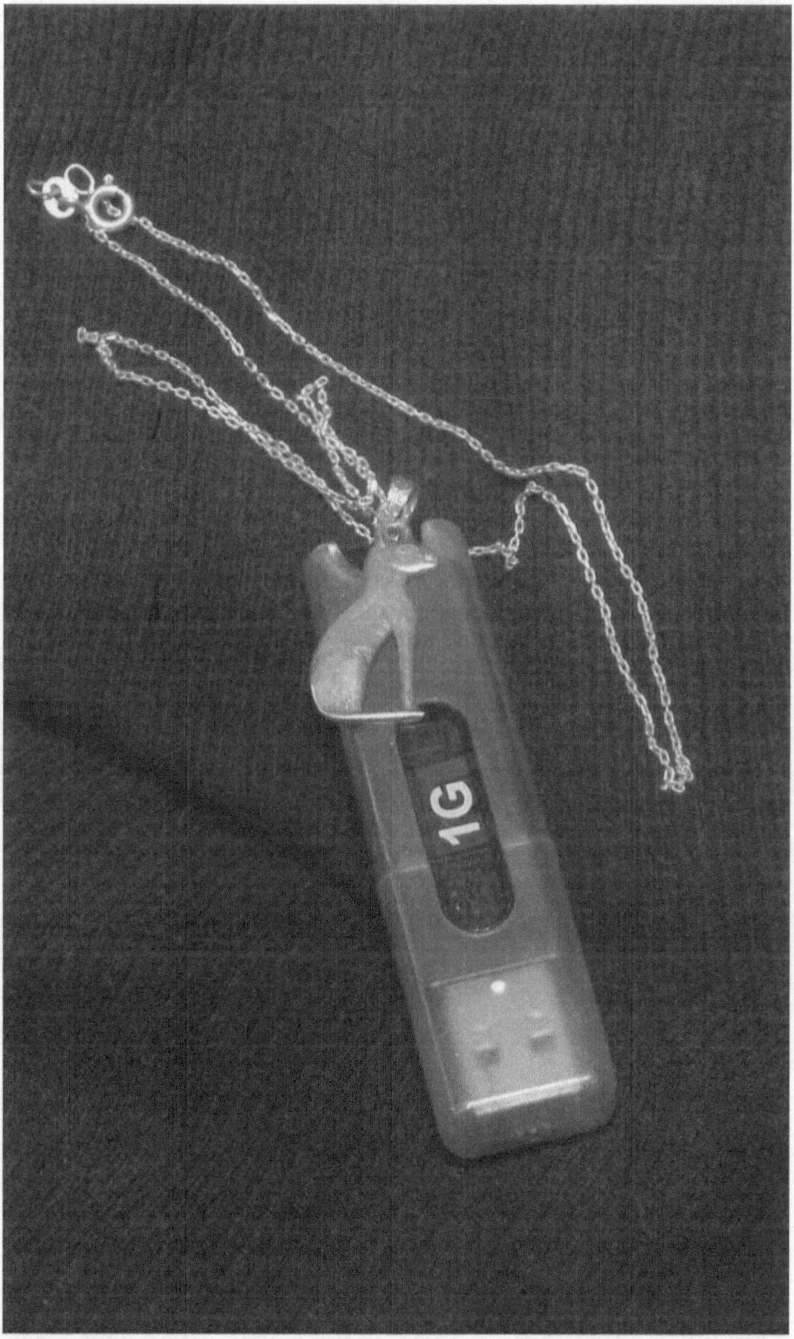

detriment the year before, more likely to make the first move. He didn't disappoint.

Josh nimbly ducked the roundhouse punch aimed at his head and lashed out with a kick of his own. The kick landed just above Koulikov's right knee. That leg had an unfortunate encounter with a limestone stele in their last confrontation. He was hoping it would be a vulnerable spot. Even at his age, Vasily Yurikovich didn't have many.

To Katzen's relief, Koulikov howled and collapsed to the stubbly ground clutching his leg. To Katzen's displeasure, he lost his own footing on the uneven ground and landed hard on his back. The star showers behind his eyes cleared just in time to see Bukharin launch himself in a flying bodyslam. Josh brought his feet up and caught the stocky ex-KGB officer in the middle and rolled him over into the ground head-first, then sprang back into a crouch ready to counter the next move.

Behind them, the trailer park was coming alive. Bear and several other dogs were setting up a tune. Doors opened and curtains were drawn back, sending faint fingers of light toward the cornfield.

"You guys should have listened to me when I told you to get lost," he hissed.

From somewhere at the edge of the cornfield, Sammie Longbaugh shouted, "You damned kids. I told you what would happen the next time you caused a ruckus out here." Then the night was shattered by a loud BANG and the wide muzzle flash of a shotgun. The Russians tore back through the cornfield, trailing colorful Slavic expletives, but Katzen didn't have time to appreciate their artistry. He was too busy keeping to shadows and making for Connor's patio. He got there just in time to grab his coffee cup and open the door as if he were stepping out instead of in, when Del, Tina and Bud came around. A flock of siren-screams edged into hearing and drew steadily closer.

"Dang it! I was afraid she'd get that old blunderbuss out again," Del groused.

Bud hawked and spat. "Somebody oughta take that thing away from her."

Del chuckled. "You gonna try?"

Bud shifted uncomfortably as the sirens and their accompanying flashing lights poured into the Park. Tina sighed. "You okay, Josh? I

promise this sort of thing don't happen all the time. The kids tear up in that field over there and Sammie takes it personal."

He sipped at the cold coffee and brushed the front of his sweater. The thumbdrive was still there. Good. He hoped he didn't have too much grass and dirt on him, he wanted to avoid a lot of questions. "Wow! That was Sammie? It sounded like an artillery division. What the hell was she using?"

"Pump shotgun. She fires it in the air usually, but the cops take a dim view of it." She paused and regarded the flotilla of officialdom. "Looks like the whole park called this time."

Bud laughed, and said with barely concealed admiration, "Well, it did sound like a worse fight than usual. When that one fella started yammerin' ... somebody musta thumped him good!"

Josh joined in the laugh, but hung back near Connor's patio while Chicago's finest took statements and read Sammie the riot act. Several other officers scoured the cornfield with flashlights. From their attitude it was business as usual.

In the distance, another altercation threatened as the CPD Officer in Charge confiscated Sammie's shotgun. At the same time, a couple of suspiciously official-looking men skirted the crowd and headed toward where Katzen leaned against the patio awning post. They strolled up with a studied casualness that screamed *fed* to Josh.

The shorter of the two said, "Looks like you folks had some excitement here tonight."

"Yeah, you guys missed it. Some kids had a brawl in the field over there. Got the whole neighborhood stirred up big time."

"Uh huh." The man watched the CPD OIC gently but firmly send Sammie back to her trailer shotgunless, then asked, "Would you be Joshua Katzen?"

"That would be me, yes," Josh answered. He was wary but trying not to show it. He never liked government types sniffing him up – even when they worked for the same boss.

The two men relaxed a little. The talker pulled an ID case out and opened it to Katzen. He read National Security Agency over the man's name in the dim light. Without waiting for a response, the agent continued, "We had a call from Dr. Connor McCrae tonight letting us know about his change in plans. He said you might have something

for us?"

Josh grinned, pulled the chain out and slid the thumbdrive off. Placing it in the agent's hand, he said, "There ya go."

The man looked at the small device. "This is the thing?"

"Connor says so. I trust him. I know from nothing about this stuff."

The talker nodded to his silent companion and, with a polite goodnight, they strolled away. Before they were out of earshot, Josh heard them muttering about dealing with amateurs.

Josh allowed himself a private laugh, then sipped at the coffee again. Feh. Cold. He dumped it out on the ground and returned inside for a fresh cup from the thermos.

Next day, Josh was back at the trailer early. He'd made a good start on the kitchen when Avi Rosenberg poked his head in the open doorway.

"Hey, Josh. When are the men in black supposed to show?"

Josh stuffed a handful of fast food sandwich wrappers into a trash bag. "Oh, they came last night. Connor called and told them the deal, so they came early."

When Avi eased himself into the living room, he filled the available space. Avi was a true giant and at nearly eight feet tall, the muscular archaeologist had to bend double to clear the low ceiling. He shot his friend a puzzled look. "Then why are you here?"

Josh swept a hand encompassing the still-wrecked kitchen and partially cleaned living room. "What? And let our friend come home to this? It's no wonder he gets so many infections."

Avi took it in and nodded slowly. "You have a point."

Josh tossed a roll of garbage bags at him. "Glad you see it my way. The bags go out the door when they're full and Bud – that's the guy in seven – hauls them off when the pile gets too high." He turned back to stuffing trash into the plastic bag, then looked up to add, "Think of it as a midden excavation."

Rosenberg laughed and peeled off a garbage bag.

Night Diet
by
J. Baumgartle

The vampire was sad, an outsider;
—of course he was also a biter;
no one came to his castle
because of the hassle
of leaving perceptibly lighter.

And yet one respectable maiden
came forth with her arms heavy laden;
her cooking was such
it delighted him much
to eat whatever she bade him.

In time others ventured there with her
to share conversation and dinner;
though she passes inspection
with rosy reflection
the Count is looking much thinner.

Never Again !
by
Glenda Mills

I was one of the most computer-illiterate people I knew, blissfully ignorant of the Internet and totally content to use my computer as a word processor and a means to send and retrieve e-mail. I was, at least, until September, 2006.

My descent into technological purgatory actually began in August of that year, when I returned to my job as a tutor at a local children's home. At the end of the second week of school, I was told that the state had changed the requirements of my job description. To keep my position, I had to have a college degree – no problem – in education – still no problem – and a current teaching license – big problem. Mine had expired two years prior, and I'd never gotten around to taking the six college credits I needed to get it renewed.

Now what? It was mid-August. The fall education classes were full. Maybe the state would grant a grace period. After all, it wasn't my fault they had changed the rules, right? Wrong. They weren't going to budge. Despite my pleading, compromise was not an option. The children's home had to have the funding from the school to pay me and Stephanie, the other tutor, for our services. The school system had to have the state money, and the state did not consider Stephanie – who also had let her license lapse – or me to be qualified. Everyone involved on the local level expressed regret over our plight, but their hands were tied by the state's purse strings. The tutoring positions were to be posted the next week.

At this juncture, Stephanie got the bright idea that we should look on-line. We found a place where we could earn six credit hours by taking two three-week classes. If we overlapped them, we could have our credits in four weeks. Back to the school administration we went, armed with this new information.

Finally, we reached an agreement. The jobs would be posted as temporary positions. Once Stephanie and I got our licenses current, we were guaranteed reinstatement. This last part was critical because the on-line classes cost $600 each. Neither one of us could afford to spend that much money unless we knew we had jobs to go back to.

Stephanie and I signed up for the same two courses so we could help each other. The first day of class, the assignment was to log on in the classroom folder and write a short biography so everyone could get to know each other. I successfully completed both tasks. For the next two weeks, I navigated through folders, found the class syllabus and my textbook, and learned how to post assignments and participate in class discussion. Maybe this wasn't going to be so bad after all.

The fragile bubble of security enveloping me burst Friday evening. I wasn't able to get to the library during the day to work on my class. I figured, no problem. I would use my husband's office computer later that night. I followed the same steps I had taken on the other days and found myself blocked from all the class folders. Remember, my skill level did not allow me to improvise. Novice that I am, I decided to call tech support. A very patient voice led me through a series of commands which I could not possibly have repeated if my life depended on it. When I had done everything he said, the same message appeared, informing me that I was still blocked from my class. The patient voice found this interesting. I had other adjectives in mind. Obviously, something was wrong with my husband's computer. At least that was the conclusion the voice came to. The solution was simple. All I needed to do was reinstall Windows, and the problem would go away. There were only a few minor flaws in this plan: I had no idea where the disc containing Windows was, it wasn't my computer, and I didn't have time for divorce proceedings. I thanked the nice voice and left.

When I got home, I decided to give my class one more go. Using my daughter's laptop, I logged on, but got the same message as before. I called tech support again, and a different patient voice led me through the same maze but, this time, it worked. Now I could get something done, in theory anyway. The reality was that it was late and I was too tired to spend much time on schoolwork. I had an assignment due the next day, but it was small. I went to bed, reasoning that I would go to the library the next morning and do it there.

I arrived at the library bright and early Saturday, prepared to type my assignment up quickly, post it, and be home within an hour. My oldest son had an out-of-town soccer game that day, and my mother and I were going together. She was meeting me at my house at 10:00.

I sat down at the computer and went through the same routine I had every other day that week, only to discover that the changes the tech support person had made to my classroom folders the night before now made it impossible for me to access them without Outlook Express, a program which was not available on any of the library computers. In a panic, I called Stephanie to see if I could post my assignment from her home computer later that evening after I got back from the soccer game. She said I could. Relieved, I went on with my day.

That evening, I used Stephanie's computer to post my assignment, assuming the crisis had passed. The next day, Stephanie got an e-mail from our professor. She said she didn't mind me posting from Stef's computer, but to make sure I signed in using my own information. Apparently, even though I did sign in as me, the assignment came through under Stephanie's name.

At this point, my computer options were running low. I couldn't even access the Internet from my PC, my daughter's laptop did not reside at my home on a reliably regular basis, the library didn't have Outlook Express, and Stephanie's computer wanted to take credit for my work. With only a couple of days left until the beginning of my second class, I went to a local university, obtained a user name and password, and got back on track.

On Tuesday, the second class started – adolescent psychology. Since I had two teenagers in the house, I was living this class. I figured my life experience, coupled with my ability to shovel the proverbial manure when necessary, would make this an easy three credits.

The first few days were busier because I had two classes to keep up with, but they went relatively well. Then came the due date for the first psychology assignment. For this class, assignments had to be posted in a read-only folder that only the professor could access. Posts in this folder did not show up immediately, so confirmation could take hours. My first attempt to send my assignment failed. By the time I realized it hadn't gone through, found out from yet another patient voice at tech support how to post in the folder correctly, and resubmitted the paper, it was late and I lost points for missing the due date. I wasn't happy, but I knew I could correctly submit assignments for the remainder of the class. With my new skill mastered and my delusion bubble mended, I entered the third week of instruction.

The third week was actually the last week of my first class. I posted my final project, logged out of that class, posted a psych assignment, and went home. One more week, and I could spend time with my children again – maybe do laundry or wash dishes.

Early the next week, I received an e-mail from the professor of my first class that read, "Did you mean to post this in my class?" and attached to the question was the psychology assignment I thought I had submitted the week before. I sent a lengthy message, along with my wayward paper, to my psychology teacher, explained my error and lost points for turning in my work late. By now, I was somewhat concerned. There were only 100 points available for the entire class, and I was nickel and diming my total with my mistakes. However, I reasoned that the other class was finished so this same thing could not happen again.

For some inane reason, both of my classes had group assignments. In my first class, critical thinking, we chose which team we wanted to be on, so Stephanie and I signed up on the same one. This meant that at least half of my group was personally accessible. The assignments were papers in various forms and on differing topics. On our team, we took turns being the one who drafted and submitted the final paper based on ideas and information provided by everyone in the group. It was a very manageable system.

For the psychology class, our learning teams were chosen by the professor, and Stephanie was not in my group. There was really only one team assignment. We had to design a school, complete with architecture, curriculum, extra-curricular activities, demographics, and parental/neighborhood involvement. As if the scope of the assignment wasn't difficult enough to accomplish, the presentation had to be done in Power Point. Power what? My husband offered to teach me, but there wasn't time in my schedule or available space in my brain for a crash course. I posted a brief explanation of my computer ineptness along with some ideas I had for the project. A couple of days before the assignment was due, I got a message from another group member requesting that everyone submit slides to be used for the presentation. I replied with a reminder that I didn't know how to do Power Point, but I hoped my previous list of ideas would be helpful. Later that week, the professor sent us our points for the project. To my horror, I

discovered that I had received a zero because I did not participate. I went back through the group discussion thread, looking for the list of ideas I had submitted. I couldn't find it. Apparently, after typing my lengthy, well-thought-out entry, I exited the folder without posting it. As far as my professor could tell, I had done absolutely nothing to help my group.

Now I was really in a panic. I sent my teacher an e-mail explaining that I had, in fact, tried to participate in the discussion, even though there was no way for me to prove it. By this point, I had become the kid in class whose dog had eaten her homework three times. I did not get a response from my professor, and the zero stood. The group project was worth 20 points. I had only received partial credit for the first week of class discussion because I had not contributed substantially to the discussion thread on at least four different days. Then there were the two late papers, both of which had been completed and "submitted" on time. I had given a gallant effort, but the best I could hope for, provided I earned all my points on my final project, was a C-. There had been numerous occasions when Stephanie and I had reminded each other that it didn't matter what our grades were. All we had to do was pass the classes and get our six credits. Suddenly, that thought was not at all comforting. I knew I would have to enter the witness protection program and obtain an entirely new identity if my husband found out I had failed the class and cost us $600 in the process, and failure was looking more and more possible.

I worked especially hard on my final project and felt really good about it when it was finished. I honestly believed I would get full credit and escape the class with a passing grade. The day I submitted it, I called tech support as soon as I got home to make sure it had posted in the read-only folder. I waited while he looked and looked and looked again, but as far as he could tell, the assignment wasn't there. He reminded me that it usually took a period of time for confirmation so I should check back later. I didn't know whether to cry, scream, or curl up in a fetal position and suck my thumb. The university library was only going to be open for a few more hours. It was the last day of class. If the post didn't show up in the folder, I would fail for sure. Out of total desperation, I called my professor's office and spoke with her in person. She told me that she did, in fact,

have my paper. After I hung up with her, I received a call from the technician I had spoken with earlier. He had found my project after all and wanted to let me know it was in the correct folder. There was nothing left to do but wait for grades to be posted the next week.

While I waited to learn my fate, I did something I rarely do – I cleaned the inside of my car, a process which always includes throwing away all the old mail, unread newspapers, french fry wrappers, chicken nugget boxes and other sundry items strewn throughout. I consider the condition of my car to be a matter of survival. If I were ever stranded, I could live off the crumbs on my seats for at least a week, thus precluding any chance of starvation. However, occasionally even I can't stand the mess any more and everything gets pitched.

I had purchased a parking pass when I first started going to the university library to work on my classes. So far, the campus police had not ticketed me, even though the pass was only good for one day, and I had used it for three weeks. It wasn't that I was cheap. I just never had the cash for a new pass not did I have coins for the metered spaces. Such was the case on the day I went to get my final grade for my psychology class. The only difference was that not only was I without change; I was also missing my lucky pass, an inadvertent victim of my uncluttered car. I catalogued the event as yet another reason why cleaning was a bad idea. I might throw away something important that had nestled its way into the bed of trash surrounding it. I knew I would only be in the library for a few minutes, so I parked anyway. What were the chances that I would get caught this time when I had spent hours parked illegally in the past weeks?

Once inside the library, I logged on and accessed my grade for my final project. Apparently, my professor had not been nearly as impressed with my work as I had been. She had deducted seven points from my score, which left me with a D- in the class. I had passed, but there was no sense of joy or relief, just an overwhelming feeling of failure and frustration. I had done very well in my first class, and I knew I had given the psychology class my best effort. Still, as I looked at my grade, the only thing I could focus on was the fact that this would be part of my academic record for the rest of my life. I sat in front of the computer screen in silence for a few minutes, logged off for the last time, and swore I would never, ever do an on-line class

again.

When I got back to my car, there was an orange ticket under the windshield wiper. Not only had I received a citation for parking without a permit, but the kind officer had also written me up for encroachment because the front of my car was an inch or so over the line of my parking space. The ticket was for $20. As I looked over the violation, I discovered a truly enlightening fact. Had I chosen to park in a space without putting money in the meter, my infraction would only have cost me $4. As I stood there, the orange paper in my hand, I once again swore with even more fervor to never, under any circumstances, take another class on-line.

Song From Beginning to (No) Ending
by
LM Harmon

In the beginning
Beginning
Beginning
I was just being
A being
One being
But feelers were feeling
And feeling
And feeling
And edges were peeling
And pealing
And feeling
So then I was growing
Dividing
And growing
Parts for feeding
Or knowing
Or rolling
Then fibers,
Nerve centers,
Growing,
Growing,
Along came the water,
The floating, the floating.
Bumping and breathing and growing
And growing
I needed the fins
For controlling the flowing
I needed the gills for the breath
And the blowing
No eyelids
No tastebuds
Just growing and going.

Green life called from dry peaks
Growing and growing
On the edge of the going,
It called
"Come and seek me!"
and feet were below-ing
below and beneath
in the silt and the soil
mud into dry land
awake in the morning
The breeze on my skin!
Drying!
Surprising!
Shaking and writhing,
Climbing and climbing.

Gills into lungs and the breathing,
The blowing!
Feet into knees into legs and still growing!
Sunlight on skin
And comes hair, growing, flowing.
Fur and dense curls and toenails and
Still growing.

Music in concert, the sounds of trees blowing,
Water on rocks,
Birds on wing crowing
Creatures tender and sweet,
Cattle lowing,
And growing and growing
On the edge, and upgoing.

Still needing and growing,
Pelts for wearing or owing,
Huts and villages too full,
Time for going.
Countrysides, seasides, filled to overflowing,
Once again in the water but this time it's rowing.

A new land, a new way,
New people for knowing.
Battles and wars and disease
But still growing.
Settle, invent, sell and harvest and sewing.
Onward and upward and into the knowing.
Sleeping and leisure and petty horn-blowing –
Keep going, keep growing,
On the edge, don't stop rolling!

Typing and talking and reading and writing,
Minds autopiloting – no, no, and no-ing!
Crack new synapses, be still and start knowing,
Open your heart to the new message growing.
Open and open and open and open,
Receive and receive, filter and throwing
Glow and be warm and then give, but *keep going*!

Write it and share it and read it and sing.
From the beginning, to the (never) ending.

The Inheritance
By
Jane E. Jones

Jory pulled off the highway and again tried to make sense of the map that the lawyer had given her. She re-read the letter for what must have been the hundredth time. It said that her great-uncle Jebediah had died and left his entire estate — a small ranch, seventeen cattle, two horses, and $2,042.15 in cash — to his grand-niece, Michelle Jordan Brown. Jory vaguely remembered seeing her father's uncle when she was very young, before her widowed mother remarried and they moved to Chicago. She hadn't seen or heard from him since and wondered why he had left his things to her. When she called, her mom told her that she had written to him occasionally. She said he had no other blood relatives and had always thought Jory was special. Jory wondered why, if he thought she was so great, he hadn't ever written to her. She had forgotten he even existed until she received the lawyer's letter. But it couldn't have come at a more opportune time — she hated her job, AND she'd just caught her boyfriend with her next-door neighbor.

On impulse, she wrote Mr. Cheatham, the lawyer, that she would be at his office in Pueblo, Colorado, the next week. Thirty-six hours later, she had quit her job, cleaned out her savings account, packed her clothes, and was headed west. Her mother had a fit, but she hadn't paid any attention to her. She was twenty-five years old for Pete's sake, plenty old enough to take care of herself.

It was obvious that Mr. Cheatham hadn't really expected her, but he had quickly gotten the papers together and soon she was on her way to Stitch, Colorado, population 127.

She found Stitch, finally, all five buildings and eighteen houses of it. There was a general store which had gas, groceries, and the post office; a ranch supply, feed and hardware store; a restaurant; a saloon/pool hall; and a church. The lady at the general store, a petite redhead about fifty years old, introduced herself as Mabel Jones and welcomed her enthusiastically. She gave Jory directions to Uncle Jeb's place.

The directions said this was it, but they had to be wrong. The place was a disaster. The log cabin had been built right up against the

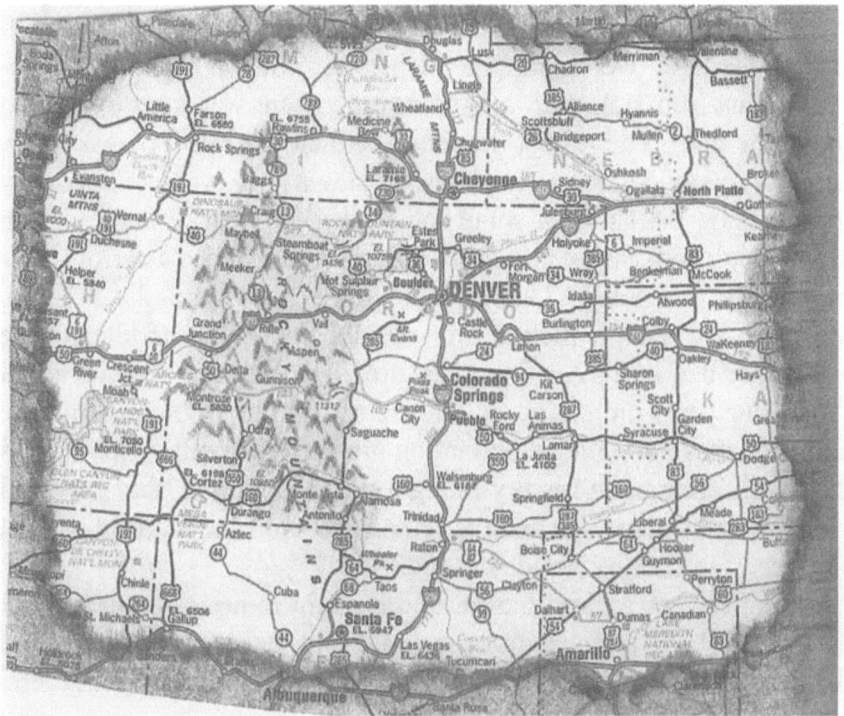

rock wall of the canyon. She thought it a wonder a big boulder hadn't fallen and smashed it. The porch sagged badly and was missing a step. The screen door hung on one hinge. A crack in the window had been patched with duct tape. The barn was in better shape than the cabin, but it was a wreck, too. There was an outhouse at the side of the cabin. None of them had ever seen a paint brush.

Jory stared in horror at her inheritance. How was she supposed to live in a place like this? Her great-uncle had been an old man, but still, you'd think he would've tried to keep it up. Finally she sighed and opened the VW Bug's door. It was too late to go back to Pueblo, and she was certain there wasn't a hotel in Stitch. The cabin would have to do for tonight, anyway. Maybe it was better inside.

It wasn't. The door opened into an L-shaped room which contained the kitchen and living room. There was another small room in the back corner. There was a wood-burning cookstove, and a hand-made table with two chairs. The dishes and pots sat on open shelves over a cast-iron sink with a hand pump. There was a rifle hanging above the door. The rest of the room held an old roll-top desk and a sagging couch. Near the fireplace she saw a well-worn leather easy chair, beside which sat a small table with a kerosene lamp and an overflowing bookcase. The walled-off portion contained a narrow bunk and a chest of drawers. Uncle Jeb s clothes hung on nails along the wall. She saw a triple picture frame on the chest. The middle picture was of her dad in his Air Force uniform. The left side showed her at about four years old sitting on a horse in front of an older man. The right side was her college graduation picture. Tears filled her eyes as she held it. She hadn't really thought much about the person who'd been her great-uncle. He hadn't seemed real until she realized he kept pictures of his family beside his bed.

She went back to the car and brought in her suitcase and her flashlight. She lit all the lamps she could find. It was getting dark, and she wanted to be certain that everything close by knew she was there. At least she hadn't found any critters living inside. The cabin didn't look nearly as bad in the warm glow of the lamps. She squared her shoulders and looked around the room. In the morning she'd decide whether to stay or not. She would have to go through her uncle's things, a job she didn't look forward to. But right now she just wanted to curl up and cry. She was too tired to even think about eating. There was no way she was getting into that bed until she'd washed the dusty old quilt and everything else on it, so she spread her sleeping bag on the couch, blew out the lamps and crawled in, fully dressed.

The next thing Jory knew, the sun was peeking over the hill, through the window, into her eyes, and nature was calling her name loud and clear. She looked doubtfully at the outhouse but decided that was the best she was going to find. She was halfway across the yard when she heard a low, male voice coming from the barn. She'd always been more a "fight" than "flight" person and walked boldly to the

open door of the barn. She saw the back of a tall, broad-shouldered man who was talking quietly to the horse he was holding. She might not know what to do with a horse, but it was hers and she wasn't going to let anyone steal it.

"Get away from my horse," she shouted loudly.

"Holy — ." The man whirled around, automatically dropping into a fighting stance. "Lady, are you trying to get yourself killed? Don't ever sneak up on a guy like that!" he yelled.

Jory stared at him and swallowed the lump in her throat. *Golly, he looks strong.* "Get away from my horse. I won't let you steal him."

The man just shook his head in disgust. "First of all, Salinda's not a him. And second, I'm not stealing her, I'm bringing her home."

"Oh, um...."

"Look, she's been at my place ever since Jeb died. She's pregnant and I didn't want to leave her up here by herself." He shook his head again. *Gol-darned female dude!* "They told me in town last night that you'd come, so I brought her home."

Jory's face burned as she tried to think of something to say, but her mind was a complete blank.

She looked so embarrassed, he felt sorry for her. "I guess I should've let you know I was here, but I figured you'd still be asleep. It's kind of early for city folk. I was just going to drop her off and go on home. I live over that ridge yonder. Me and Jeb were friends and I was just helping out. Folks call me Trigger."

She decided to ignore that crack about sleeping late. "Trigger?"

He blushed. "Yeah. I tended to have a hair-trigger temper when I was young."

"And you're more stable now that you're so much older?"

"Yep. Old age'll do that to you."

She laughed. He couldn't be much older than she was.

He grinned at her. "Well, anyway, here's your horse, home safe and sound. Like I said, her name's Salinda. I'll put her out in the pasture for ya. She's not due to foal for a couple of months yet, and there's plenty of grass & water. She'll be all right."

"Thanks. I'm sorry I yelled at you. I appreciate your taking care of her," Jory said. "Hey, wait. They said Uncle Jeb had two horses. Where's the other one?"

"That was Tonka. He was real old — Jeb got him when he was still rodeoin'. He just up and died right after Jeb did."

"Oh. That's ...."

"Salinda, now, she's just a youngster. He bought her a couple of years ago, mostly to keep Tonka company. Horses don't like to be alone, ya know."

"I didn't know that."

"Yep, they're real social critters. Soon's I get a chance, I'll bring old Queenie over to stay with her." He patted Salinda on the neck. "Well, I've got to go or I'll be late getting to work. If ya need anything, my place is about two miles southwest of here. Just follow that path there. I reckon I'm your closest neighbor."

"Can I give you a lift back home?"

"No, thanks. Shiloh's tied out back. We led Salinda over.

"Uh, the letter said I had some cows, too. Do you know where they are?"

"Yeah, they're up in the north pasture. I've been keeping an eye on 'em. There's a good spring there, so they should be okay for a while."

He turned Salinda loose in the pasture and swung onto the big black horse waiting patiently by the gate. He touched the brim of his hat, nodded to her and disappeared up the trail.

Jory stood there staring after him, rehashing that conversation. He certainly hadn't told her much about himself. All she knew was that he was around six feet tall, muscular, had black hair, dark eyes, and looked very good in his faded jeans and denim work shirt. Oh yeah, and folks called him Trigger. Well, at least she had a neighbor, if you could call someone two miles away a neighbor. And she realized that nature was reminding her why she came outside in the first place.

Trigger urged Shiloh up the trail at a fast lope. He wanted to get away from there real bad. This was going to be a challenge and he needed to figure out how he was going to handle the problem. That girl was in for a surprise. And she had no clue yet.

Jory spent the rest of the morning packing up her Uncle Jeb's clothing and going through his things. She discovered an old leather

suitcase full of silver trophy buckles from his rodeo days. The bookcase held mostly histories of the old West and paperback murder mysteries. A wooden nail keg by the fireplace was almost full of flint axe and arrowheads. She looked in the big, old roll-top desk, but it was crammed with papers, and she decided to wait a while before she tackled it. She kept the buckles, a sheepskin-lined denim jacket that would fit her, and Jeb's run-down boots with the old spurs still on them, but put everything else into a big bag. There had to be a church or charity in Stitch that would take the clothes. Then she stuffed all the blankets and such in a garbage bag and threw them in the back of her Bug, hoping there was a laundromat somewhere in town. Sometime during the morning she'd realized she wanted to stay for a while.

It was after noon when she made the twelve-mile drive to Stitch. Mabel Jones greeted Jory as she walked into the store, chatting away about how glad she was that she had come. She told her to just leave Jeb's clothing in the room at the back of the store. Anyone was welcome to what was there whether they could pay or not. There was also a room with two washers and dryers where she could do her laundry. Mabel said that while she was waiting for her stuff to wash, she might as well come and eat lunch with her at the Grub Company, which was just across the street from the store. There, she met Kathy and her husband, Jim, who ran the restaurant and the saloon and pool hall next door. Since Mabel talked pretty-much non-stop, Jory soon learned a lot about the town and its residents.

Jory told Mabel about the shape the cabin was in, and Mabel said that her son by her first marriage — his name was Zack Blackhawk — was a whiz at fixing things. He'd probably be willing to repair the cabin and barn for her. Jory decided she could use the money she'd inherited to fix the place up good enough to stay there until the end of summer. She'd be out of money and would have to find a job somewhere before winter.

After lunch, Jory bought the groceries and cleaning supplies she needed and Mabel helped her fold up the blankets and towels from the laundry. By that time, it was late afternoon, and Mabel said that Zack would be coming to town pretty soon. "He eats his supper at the saloon and hangs out at the pool hall most nights," she told her with a, you-know-how-boys-are look.

Jory really wanted to get the cabin fixed soon, so she decided to wait until Zack got there. She sat in the back of the store talking to Mabel between customers and learning all she could about Uncle Jeb and his family, or lack thereof. Mabel said he'd talked often about his nephew, who was killed overseas in the Service, and had shown her pictures of Jory every now and then. But he'd never mentioned anyone else. "He sure was proud of you. Told us all about how you went to college and were a commercial artist now. Of course, none of us know exactly what a commercial artist does, but it sounds important. He bragged about you working for that big advertising agency in Chicago."

"Well, it might have sounded impressive, but it was the pits. The boss had a God complex — thought the whole world was supposed to run according to his rules — and he had some very strange rules. And because I was the low girl on the totem pole, I got all the crappy jobs. I really was glad to get away from that place," Jory said, and she went on to describe some of the crazy things that had happened at work. Soon they were both laughing so hard tears were running down their cheeks.

Mabel finally said she had to close up and get on to her quilting club meeting. She looked out and said Zack's truck was sitting in front of the pool hall.

Jory said goodnight and stepped out onto the wooden sidewalk. She was surprised to find that it was almost dark. She'd been enjoying herself so much she hadn't realized how late it was. She went across the street and stepped into the saloon, blinking at the smokey haze hanging in the air. She looked around in amusement. It actually looked like the saloons in the old western movies, except there were no dance-hall girls, just a bunch of men in cowboy hats, sitting around, talking and playing cards. As she made her way to the bar, she could hear the distinctive clank of pool balls colliding in another room. She asked the bartender if Zack Blackhawk was there. He turned to the door at the end of the bar and yelled, "Hey, Blackhawk, git out here, ya got a lady lookin fur ya."

Jory heard a gruff male voice yell back, "I don't know any ladies, Max." And another voice said, "You better hit the back door, pal, she's probably gonna tell you you're a daddy!" and several others laughed.

She was blushing furiously when the door swung open and Trigger stepped through. He paused when he saw Jory, then sauntered across the wood floor, his spurs jingling. He swept off his hat with a flourish. "Well, it appears I do know a lady after all. How-do, Ms. Brown, ma'am. What kin I do for ya?"

She just stared at him a moment. "Uh, Mabel Jones said her son did repair work. Are you Zack?" She was having trouble imagining tiny, redheaded Mabel Jones as the mother of this towering dark-haired man.

"You need something repaired, do ya?"

He was laughing at her, she realized, and that was just what she needed to get her brain working again. "You've seen that place! Of course I need something repaired. But if it's too big a job for you, or if you don't want the work, I'll get someone else," she snapped.

His grin grew even wider. "Well, workin's not one of my favorite things, but I am partial to eating, so I reckon I could fix the place up some. I'll need another day to finish with the spring round-up for the Double U, then I can start, if ya want."

"That will be fine. Thank you." Jory turned and made a hasty retreat. She didn't know why she ended up feeling like a silly kid every time she talked to that annoying man, but she just wanted to get away from him before she made a fool of herself again.

Max walked up beside him. "That her?"
"Yep."
"Pretty girl. What're ya gonna do?"
Trigger slapped his hat against his leg and shook his head. "Play the hand out, pal. That's all I can do."
"I reckon. Good luck."
"Thanks. I think I'm gonna need it."

Two days later, Trigger drove his pickup truck into the front yard and parked under the big cottonwood tree. The truck bed was piled with lumber, blocks, tools, ladders, and a bunch of stuff that Jory didn't recognize. He climbed out of the truck and touched his finger to his hat brim. "Zachary Dakota Blackhawk reporting for duty, ma'am. Whatcha want me to do first?"

"Stop calling me ma'am; my name's Jory. And I don't have a clue where you should start. I mean, look at this place. What do you think?"

"Well, ma – uh, Jory," he glanced around, "I'd guess we'd better start with that porch. You might break a leg on it and then I'd have to shoot ya."

She laughed. "Okay. I'll let you get to it then. I'm still sorting out the inside. Yell if you need anything."

"Right." Without another word, he turned to unload the truck. Before long, he was stripped to the waist as he carried concrete blocks and lumber over to shore up the sagging porch.

Jory glanced out the window every little bit, and watched him at work. She finally went out to offer him a glass of iced tea, which he accepted gladly. At noon, she made tuna salad sandwiches and brought them and potato chips and more iced tea outside. They sat on the truck's tailgate in the shade and ate their lunch. She told him about Chicago, and he talked about growing up in the mountains and spending time with his father's people on the reservation. Their backgrounds were so different and they each wanted to hear about the other's life. Finally, Trigger forced himself to go back to work and Jory went in to mop the floors. The next day, he finished the porch and re-hung the door. He measured the broken window and left early to order its replacement.

After he left, Jory tried to concentrate on cleaning the cabin, but soon gave up. It was just too boring. She tried picking up the yard — gave up on that. She tried straightening out the tack room in the barn — gave up on that. She missed Trigger's hammering and banging on things. It was just too quiet here by herself. Okay, she admitted, she was lonesome. That was something she hadn't expected. The whole reason for coming out here was to get away from people.

Finally, she went inside, lit a kerosene lamp against the shadows, and turned her transistor radio on loud. She settled in to sort through the papers in Jeb's old roll-top desk. That ought to keep her busy for a while.

Trigger drove to the hardware store to order the new window, then stopped at the grocery. Mabel gave him a hug and asked how things were going out at Jory's place. He told her about the work he'd

done and what he had planned next. She gave him a look. "You know what I mean."

He sighed. "Mom, there's nothing to tell. I've only been there two days. Give me a chance, doggone it."

She got a far-away look in her eyes. "That's all your pa needed. He didn't waste any time, no sirree."

"Mom!"

Mabel laughed at him. "I may be old now, junior, but I used to be quite a gal, ya know."

"You're still beautiful," he said, giving her a big hug. Then he frowned. "But, what am I supposed to do? I can't just walk up and tell her that I'm part of her inheritance. I mean, if I tell her what Jeb said, she'll run me clear off the place."

"Probably. You might tell her you've had a crush on her for more than twenty years."

"I have not!" He declared, then grinned at her. "Well, maybe a little. But I don't think that would be a good idea either." He sighed. "We'll see how it goes."

Jory sifted and sorted through bills, receipts, and rodeo flyers until she was about ready to just scoop everything into the trash. But still, she began to get a feel for her great-uncle and his life. Then she found a gold mine. The bottom drawer had a bundle of letters from her dad, tied with baling twine. There was another bunch of letters from her mom, and a box with lots and lots of pictures all scrambled together. She carried the drawer to the kitchen table and read the letters her dad had written to his uncle. By the time she got to the last one, tears were running down her cheeks. The letters began when her dad was just a teenager and ended with a copy of the notice from the Department of Defense advising of his death. She tied them back up in their baling twine and held them for a while as she tried to remember the man who had been her father. She couldn't even see him any more. Maybe he was in some of the pictures. She yawned and glanced at the old mantle clock above the fireplace, sitting up in surprise to find it was past midnight. The rest would have to wait until tomorrow.

She awoke as Trigger's pickup rumbled and rattled down the hill. She jumped up, quickly got dressed and met him just as he stepped

up on the porch. She didn't want him to know she'd just gotten up. He would tease her mercilessly about how city folk slept half the day away.

But it didn't work. He grinned and said innocently, "Had a short night, did ya?"

"How did you know?"

"Well, maybe because your hair looks like you stuck your finger in a light socket, or it could be that you don't have the coffee ready yet. That's grounds for a labor strike, ya know."

"Ha, ha. Very funny. Come in here, I want to show you something." She showed him the treasure she'd found the night before. "These are from my dad to Uncle Jeb. I sat up and read them until after midnight. Dad's been gone so long, I can't even remember him. They're helping me recall a little."

"That's good. I'm glad Jeb kept them. Um, did you find anything else?"

"There's some letters from my mom, too, and some old pictures; but I haven't looked at them yet." She headed to the kitchen and poked at the fire in the stove. "I'll have you some coffee in just a few minutes — can't have the workers walking out, can we?" She put the coffee pot on the stove. "I really wish I had a refrigerator. The Styrofoam cooler is about out of ice. The thing I miss most is my cold Dr. Pepper for breakfast."

He gave her a wide-eyed look. "Dr. Pepper for breakfast? You city-folk really are weird. Why didn't you put it in the cold room?"

"What's a cold room? Nobody told me I had one."

"I'm sorry, I thought you knew. It's right over here. I've never been in it, but I've seen Jeb get things out." He went to the back of the cabin and lifted the Indian blanket that hung on the wall, revealing a door. It opened into cool darkness. "This's why the cabin was built against the cliff. There's a natural cave that goes back into the hillside. I think in the old days it may have been used to hide from Indians and such, but anyhow, it's always cool in there. The temperature stays around 50 degrees, no matter how hot it gets outside." He lit the lantern that was hanging just inside the door and raised it above his head. The light showed a set of shelves with canned goods and an old-fashioned icebox at one side of a tunnel disappearing into the darkness.

Jory looked around in wonder. She had never even suspected this was here. "How far back does the cave go?"

"Jeb never said. Maybe we can explore it sometime."

"Uh, maybe. But not today, we've both got stuff to do."

Trigger laughed. "You're chicken, aren't you?"

Jory blushed. "Yes. I don't like dark places."

"Okay. Some day I'll give it a look if ya want. But now I need to get that window in before it rains."

"The man on the radio didn't say anything about rain."

"Yeah, but he doesn't live out here. Trust me, it'll storm before night. If you're scared of storms, you can come over to my place."

"No, I'm not afraid of storms. I'll be fine here."

He looked a little disappointed. "Okay, if you're sure." He grabbed up a mug, poured his coffee and headed for the door. "Better get busy then."

Jory watched him unload the window frame and then went to look at the letters again. She glanced at a few of her mother's letters, but they didn't interest her very much. She sorted through the pictures, and found several of her dad and her mother and even a couple of her as a baby.

At the very bottom of the drawer was a white envelope, and when she turned it over, it had her name written on it. She eagerly opened it and pulled out a piece of notebook paper.

Her breath caught when she unfolded it. It was a letter from her great-uncle.

Howdy, Jory.

It's good to talk to you. I've started many letters, but never did finish any of them. Guess you're wondering why I'm doing this now. Well, I guess I just wanted to say hi and let you know how proud I am of you. I'm not much for mushy stuff, so that's all I'll say about that.

Mostly I wanted to say I'm glad you've got the ranch and I hope you decide to keep it. It's a fine place, and you've got some real nice folks for neighbors. They won't bother you any, but they'll come a runnin if you need help, especially Trigger. He's a good man and a hard worker, can repair anything you

need. He used to get real aggravated cause I wouldn't let him fix things around here.

There's a picture in the envelope with this letter. It was taken the last time you were here. I don't reckon you remember that far back, so I wanted to remind you. You were just barely four years old, and you wandered off and got lost. Your mother and me searched all around, but we couldn't find you. So I sent her over to my neighbor Rocky's place to ask for help. Well, him and his boy rode right over. The boy must'a been around six at the time. We were ready to scatter and hunt for you; but that boy now, he just sat there on his horse and cocked his head sideways. I asked Rocky what he was doin, and Rocky said that he was listening to the land, that it told him things. Well, I figured he was just giving me some of that Indian talk, him being a full-blooded Ute. But then the boy kicked his horse in the side and took off at a gallop down the canyon, and Rocky said we should follow his boy. I thought it was dumb for us all to go the same way, but we'd tried everything else, so we all started down the trail. We'd only gone about a mile when here comes that little boy back, holding you in front of him on the saddle. When he got to us, we tried to take you down, but you started crying and holding onto him, and he said to leave you alone, that he'd bring you in, and that's what he did. Well, you followed him around the rest of the time youall were here and pitched a fit any time he got out of your sight. He sure missed you bad when you went home. Your mom took this-here picture, and I hope you remember.

It wasn't long after that your mama married that other fella and moved you away to the big city, and we haven't seen either of you since. Your mama kept writing to me though and sending pictures, and you tell her I'm mighty grateful for that. Well, that's all I've got to say. You be happy.

Uncle Jeb

Jory swallowed the lump in her throat and pulled the picture out of the envelope.

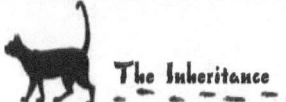 

She sat there and stared at herself sitting on a horse in front of a little dark-haired boy. He had his arms around her and was grinning for all he was worth. She whispered one word, "Trigger."

Just then he came through the door and she quickly covered the picture.

"Well, that's all done. You want me to fix something else?"

Jory just grinned. She understood now why her uncle had let the place get so bad. There was a lot that needed Trigger to fix it. Yes, she was sure there would always be something.

Orcharditis

by

J. Baumgartle

Dad loves planting fruit trees
regardless of the hundred plums
on the hillside
between pines and cedars,

regardless of the hundred plums
dripping aged fruit
between pines and cedars
for wasps and bees,

dripping aged fruit
you can't approach
for wasps and bees,
incipient pollinators

you can't approach
except in the rain.
Incipient pollinators
will nab apples and pears,

except, in the rain,
our sting-sensitive mother
will nab apples and pears,
make pies and preserves,

our sting-sensitive mother,
one eye on the window,
will make pies and preserves,
setting jars to cool,

one eye on the window
where Dad smiles and waves,
–setting jars to cool,
she waves back.

Where Dad smiles and waves
on the hillside,
she waves back.
Dad loves planting fruit trees.

Question for
THE HORSE LISTENER
Of Horse Insanity Magazine

by
Joy Kirchgessner

Dear Horse Listener:

How do you load a horse into a horse trailer? I just bought a small estate and got a free horse as a bonus. The former owner was getting stressed because he said that it would make the horse very unhappy if it had to leave its home, was there any way it could stay on the estate? That was so sad, I almost cried. He seemed truly relieved, bless his heart, when I told him I'd always wanted a horse and would love to keep it. The horse's real name is Unrule'. I think that's French. I didn't want to appear pompous, so I nicknamed him Puddin, because he's so cute. Anyway, I just bought this sweet little pink one-horse trailer. It has a door near the front and a door on the rear. The dealer sold it to me at a real bargain. He was so helpful; he even showed me how to hitch it to my KIA. I think it's time Puddin and I ventured out. Signed,

I-Am-Feeling-So-Lucky.

Dear Lucky:

If you are intent upon using this horse, please seek out an experienced equestrian who can be there with you. Preferably, *you* would be observing from 100 feet away while the experienced equestrian loads the horse. Also, read any and all horse advice material that you can get your manicured nails on. I suggest you start with my column, in the April 2006 back issue of this magazine, addressing horse name choices and their meanings. I have a feeling the name Unrule' is not of French origin.

There are as many different methods of loading a horse as necessity invents. I will mention but a few from my own experience.

First, you must have subdued your horse and have a halter and lead on it. I hope you are familiar with horse tack terminology and tack usage. If this helps, the halter is the strap looking thingy that fits

on the horse's head. There is a metal lead ring on the halter. The metal lead ring should end up under the horse's jaw and not in the middle of its forehead. You will attach a lead rope to this ring. Leading a horse from its forehead instead of under its jaw simply will not give you the control and leverage needed. Please look at any diagrams you can find. The horse should allow you to lead it when correctly fitted with this apparatus.

It would be best to park your KIA and hitched trailer inside a small fenced pen and load your horse from there. The horse may resist this trailering idea altogether, and run like it was late for a half-price sale at the local mall.

Guide him to the rear open door of the trailer. The door must be open or Puddin can't get in. If you are indeed lucky, Puddin will step up into the trailer by himself. Let the lead go and stay out of his way.

If by now you see that Puddin refuses to step one hoof in that trailer, but you are intent upon aggravating the situation, try the following methods.

In my opinion, one of the mildest techniques is 'The Lure'. The Lure is so called because the idea is to *lure* the horse inside the trailer with a treat such as an apple, corn, oats, anything it likes to eat.

Step up into the trailer with the lead rope in hand, the other end being attached to the halter which is on Puddin's head. Make sure that the front door of the trailer is open. You will need to exit through this door. Gently, offer Puddin the treat while staying just out of reach. Sweet-talk him. In your case, that could be 'Who's my big boy?'. Puddin may fake being able to get into the trailer and with neck outstretched, he reaches in as far as he can, lips quivering, big brown eyes begging. It's a touching performance in an attempt to play on your sympathy. Do not fall for this act. Conduct yourself as you would in luring a potential mate. Stay just out of reach until you have what you want.

Be cautious, as your horse may be a 'Leap-Of-Faither'. After teasing him with the treat, he could suddenly hurtle into the trailer in a single bound. There may not be room in the trailer for you and the horse both. You must be quick enough to jump out the front door and

shut it before Puddin escapes through with you.

The next method is the 'Buddy Horse System'. This one is impossible for you, as you have a one-horse trailer. This may be a clue as to why you purchased the trailer at such a discount—that, and the color pink. I will describe the method even so. Have a friend load a well-seasoned horse (This is not a cooking term.) into a more than one horse trailer and hope that your horse will go in with it. Make sure that your horse merely likes this Buddy Horse and is not sexually attracted or you will get into an entirely different set of problems. You did not say whether Puddin is a stud (balled) or a gelding (deballed—this is not French). Just to be on the safest side, do not use a female horse as a Buddy Horse.

Next is the 'Dead Pull'. I really don't recommend it as it takes more brawn than brains. By reading your question, I'm not sure if there is enough of either one. But if you really think you can pull 750 pounds or more of dead weight, then have a field day. The horse may decide that what you are trying to communicate is a playful tug-of-war and proceed to pull in the opposite direction. Defiantly, hang on to the lead rope with both hands. Puddin will probably pull you out the rear door to land in a green mushy pile of manure that he has most assuredly deposited there by now. The game is made even faster and more fun if there is green mushy manure *inside* the trailer. Traction is cut in half as you ski out the rear door.

The 'Push' is something akin to the 'Dead Pull' only you try to *push* the horse into the trailer. If the horse doesn't express its displeasure by kicking the black polka dots off your pink spandex pants, you will gradually be applying your full body pressure with your hands or shoulder to Puddin's rump. More often than not, the 'Push' results in what I describe as the 'Trip Through the Grand Canyon'. You will find yourself slowly slipping from the horse's plump cheeks and into that deep divide.

If by chance you do get Puddin into the trailer, tie your end of the lead rope to the hitching ring inside the front of the trailer. It is very important to shut the trailer doors and secure them. When riding in the trailer down the highway, he may need to lean on the rear door for balance. If the door is open, he may accidentally fall out, and not be able to keep up with your vehicle while it's traveling at any speed

over ten miles and hour.

So there you have it. Many happy trails. Look for my article in next month's issue of Horse Insanity. We will discuss how to unload a horse.

November 21, 2002

by

Bonnie L. Abraham

Let me start by saying, writer's group was to meet that night. That's important, because that's what caused the whole morning to spin out of control. When I woke up, I had two things I knew I needed to do. The first was to get copies of chapter three of my Willim story made for the writer's group. The other was to go to the grocery. Simple, right?

Since I had printed out chapter three the previous night, all I needed to do before taking off on my two little errands was to write out my grocery list. I copied the current items from the ongoing "out-of" list on the refrigerator, then went through the recipes for the things I planned to make in the next few days in preparation for Thanksgiving. With list in hand, I grabbed my purse, got in my car and took off.

At the bottom of the drive, I realized I had forgotten chapter three. I turned around in the drive across the street, drove back up the hill, ran into the house, got the story, got back into the car – throwing the story pages onto the passenger seat as I got in – and headed for the copy store.

I am a creature of habit. By the time I got from home to Main Street, (we're talking three blocks, here) I was locked into go-to-the-grocery mode and forgot to stop at the copy store. I realized this when I saw the pages in the passenger seat as I got out of the car at the grocery. *No problem,* I thought, *I'll just stop on the way home.*

I got inside the grocery and realized I didn't have my grocery list. *Now how did I manage to forget that? I was working on it just before I left.*

This was a problem. There were several items on the list that I didn't normally buy, and I knew I was going to forget something. Determined not to go back home again to get the list, I trudged up and down each aisle of the grocery, hoping to jog my memory in the process.

It didn't work. As I was paying for my groceries, I remembered *butter. Well, that can wait. I am not going back for it.* I finished checking out, put the groceries in the car and drove home.

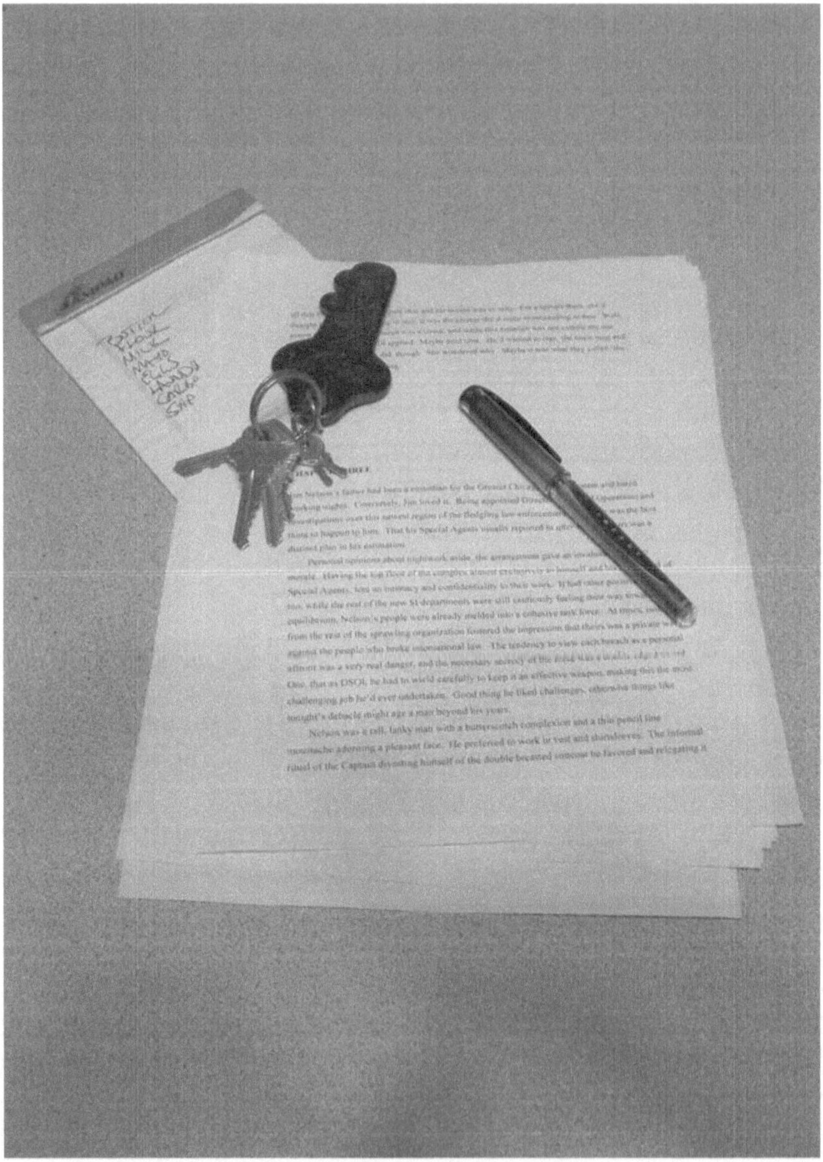

Mmm-hmm. You're sitting there asking, "But what about the copies?" But I told you, I am a creature of habit: home to grocery; grocery to home.

Once home, I grabbed my purse as I started to get out of the car, and there was the story. By then, I was more than a little irritated with myself. I picked up the pages, trying to decide if I should carry in the groceries or head back to the copy shop first – and there under the story was my shopping list.

I had forgotten three items.

I headed back to the copy shop, trying to convince myself I could do without the items I had forgotten at the grocery. Then I noticed the car was almost out of gas. The gas station I go to all the time (creature of habit, remember) is past the grocery store. *I am not happy.* Still, I didn't want to have to fill up on the way to the meeting; it was in the other direction.

I got the copies made, actually remembered to go to the gas station and headed home. As I passed the grocery, I thought, *What the heck. The morning is shot. I might as well finish the grocery list while I'm here.* It was during this trip to the grocery that I decided to get the makings for party mix to take to the meeting.

At 12:30 I pulled into my drive for the third time, thinking at least I had gotten it all done. – Or had I?

I made the party mix that afternoon and stapled the story pages together. I remembered to go to the meeting. I remembered to take the story. I forgot the party mix.

There *had* to be something!

The Ashtray
by
Teddi Robinson

I stared at the empty spot where I'd stored the souvenir ashtray from Colorado. How could they *do* this to me? *Why?* Boy! *Am I angry!* This was adding insult to injury! Not only had I lost my husband, but his children and grandchildren swiftly descended upon me like a swarm of locusts— *and* someone from his family had taken the ashtray my step-mother had given me many years ago!

Late in the 1970s, I visited my father and his new bride, Ann, in Terre Haute, Indiana, where I saw and admired the unique ashtray. It was a circle with sides of silver lace, the bottom, a colorful mosaic. The tile had the Colorado state flag, state bird, and the date the state was admitted to the flag spelled out in a semi-circle. Not practical or usable but *very* pretty to admire.

Handing me the souvenir, Ann said, "Before he died, my first husband gave me this ashtray. We went to Colorado to fish on our honeymoon, and he bought it for me as a token of his love. Fond memories from the past.... Could I give it to *you?*"

"Yes," I replied. "I'd appreciate that. I have the perfect spot for it in my curio cabinet." I thought of it as a special treasure from Ann's hand to mine.

The ashtray stayed in my curio cabinet for twenty-five years, until recently. It wasn't worth anything...at least I didn't *think* so. After all, it was *just* a souvenir.

I'm sure Evart's children and grandchildren thought *he'd* bought the ashtray, on a visit to Colorado sometime in the 1970s with his son, Raymond. This, I felt, to be a logical deduction.

I would've called the police, but the only thing missing was the ashtray and I was sure it wasn't worth more than ten dollars. I doubted the police would be interested in pursuing a crime of such little value. Besides, only two of the people gathered in my home were from my area. The others were from Colorado, North Carolina, Texas, and New Zealand— basically, scattered around the world. Would the police even *try* to find out who took it? I didn't think so.

Yes, the house *was* full of people. If *any* of them thought the ashtray valuable, they would've taken it. But who? Would I ever know? I doubted it. The family stuck together like glue, and if one lied the others swore it for the truth.

Let's look at the facts a minute: I married Evart in 1992. Helen, his daughter, really didn't want him to get married again. Helen's mother, Terry and Evart were divorced when Raymond was nine years old and Helen was eight. The two remained friends. But, children have long memories.... Perhaps, in their eyes, no other woman was good enough for *their* dad.

Evart had developed some health problems over the last couple of years. In August of 2004 he decided to have his hernia repaired. But, the doctor didn't repair the hernia— he'd found a growth on Evart's stomach.

Doctor Bill said, "This is either lymphoma or pancreatic cancer. I'm hoping it's lymphoma because that's much easier to treat. However, let's just tell Evart he has a tumor until we get the biopsy back Friday."

Stunned, I asked, "How long will he be in recovery?"

"About an hour," he answered. "Is there someone I can call to be with you?"

"No."

He murmured, "Are you sure you're okay?"

"Yes. I'll be back in an hour. Thank you." When I reached my car, I started to cry, because I knew this was the beginning of the end of our life. They'd found a malignant tumor on the top of Evart's head two months before. The doctor said the tumor was the kind that had roots and would spread to other parts of his body, but they thought they'd gotten the tumor before it spread. Apparently...they hadn't.

Wearily, I called the church and asked Opal, the church secretary, "Is the minister in?"

"No, Teddi," she sadly told me, "Frank just left to go home and no one else is here."

My voice broke as I asked, "Please, Opal... can you call and get him to come back? I *do* need to talk to him. I'm on my way out to the church now and should be there in about half an hour." I could hear her comforting, sad smile when she spoke. "I'll try to get in touch with Frank and have him here when you arrive."

"Okay... thanks," were all the words I could manage. I doubted I'd ever get to the church, but I finally did— Frank didn't get there until after me. I filled him in on what the Doctor had said, and Frank whispered, "Let's pray."

I felt better having talked to Frank and having the prayers said. Then it was back to the hospital. I wasn't prepared for the return visit.

The volunteer for the outpatient surgery asked me, "Are you ready to see your husband?"

"Yes, I think I am," I softly answered. "Is he still in recovery?"

"No," he said, "they took him over for a CT scan when he woke up. Someone'll be here shortly to take you to him."

Then, two nurses came and asked, "What did the doctor say?"

I told them, and one of the nurses said, "You're *not* ready to see him... are you?"

"No, I'm not," I murmured. "I'm going home for a little while. Tell him I went shopping... ran away... *anything*."

"That's the wise thing to do," she said and smiled at me. "You'll be able to talk to him, at that time. Besides— the CT scan'll take awhile."

"I'll see you later," I replied.

Somehow, I made it home. Once there, I tried to call Al, Evart's brother. After several fruitless attempts, always finding the line busy, I gave up. Finally, I sent Al and Marty an email, instead, and then I called Evart's daughter-in-law, Joyce. Thank God she was home and not on the phone. Reluctantly, I shared the sad news with my stepdaughter-in-law.

Joyce's beautiful sense of humor was a godsend. "Just think," she said, "You get to play nurse."

"Shall I dye my hair red also?"

Joyce chuckled, "I know he told you that he preferred red-heads, but he never married one. So, I wouldn't be too quick to dye my hair. Besides, what shade of red would you choose?"

"That's a very good question," I laughed in spite of my deep grief, thankful for my dear stepdaughter-in-law's distracting silliness. "Maybe a very bright red or do you think a strawberry blonde would do it?"

"I've got it!" she cried. "Have the beautician dye a streak of

each color, then Evart can help you decide."

I laughed, hard. "Sure, then I'll go to clown school, just to justify the ten colors of red in my hair!"

"That would be *my* solution," Joyce replied. "I've got to go but I'll have Raymond call this evening."

I hung up the phone and returned to the hospital.

I found Evart on a bed in the hall still waiting for the CT scan. As soon as he caught sight of me, he said, "They won't tell me a thing. What's wrong that I have to have more tests?"

"Ah... eh... well... well," I glanced around the hallway, dropped my voice to an exaggerated conspiratorial tone and continued, "they've discovered you're pregnant and they want to see if it's twins or not."

With a look of exasperation, he said, "Oh, come on, now. What *is* wrong?"

I bit the bullet and blurted out the news. "You have a tumor. They're checking to see... so they'll know how to treat you."

"A tumor?"

This turned into a very hard week. Evart told everyone he met that he had a tumor— his way of dealing with it, I suppose. Me? I knew it was cancer.

The cancer was lymphoma, stage 4. The doctor said the chemotherapy would extend his life a few months. Evart decided on the treatments.

After a year of consultations, visits to the doctor, trips to the hospital and chemo treatments, he passed away. Ashes to ashes, dust to dust... in my mind, I connected my husband's death to the monetarily worthless ashtray. I still don't know if I was angry with *him* for leaving me to deal with "his" family or more angry with the "family" who stole the ashtray.

I'll never know who took the ashtray. But the one thing I do know, they'll never get the money they hoped for it. Listed on e-Bay was an ashtray just like Ann's for $500.00. Highest bid $5.00. Perhaps I could buy it back for $6.00. But, why bother? That's just one more thing I don't have to dust.

In the Fast Lane

by

J. Baumgartle

Can't talk now. My sister-in-law just called, and she's on her way over. Let's see....twenty minutes from the airport.... Sure, I can change Ty, pick up the toys, do the dishes and shower before she gets here. Probably have time to make the beds and scrub the kitchen floor, as well.

I hesitate, groping mentally for the likeliest course of action, which whops me behind the knees and hangs on.

"Ty, come here you little hit-and-run!" I fish for my two-year-old, hoist him into a hug, and we're off to chase down a diaper. At least he didn't bite me this time.

Fifteen minutes later, the two of us have sort of showered, if the splashed-up bathroom is any indication. I jam clothes on our damp bodies and start the dishes, just as the doorbell rings.

"Look, Ty, it's Aunt Essie!" I exclaim, glad, in spite of myself, to see another human my age.

"Phyllis," she replies cheerfully, meeting my embrace. Ty is fascinated, but not yet ready to respond. I put him down, forget about how messy things look, and plunge into enjoying her visit.

She's in town to film her cooking show, The Light Fantastic. "We're doing lunches," she tells me, and wants to cook one, here, to get my opinion.

"There may not be enough ingredients, Essie; we're running low on groceries. I've been meaning to get out...."

"If you've got some flour tortillas, I think we're in business," she remarks, while investigating the contents of the refrigerator.

Ty laughs as she peek-a-boos him from behind its door.

Then we are into a flurry of wilted lettuce and sauteed pineapple, and lunch is on the table.

"I'm surprised you weren't out of tortillas, the way Greg eats them up," Essie comments, as we settle ourselves at the table.

"I thought he preferred sandwiches to wraps," I return, startled.

"My brother has really changed, then," she says, in a this-cannot-possibly-be-true voice. "What convinced you of that?"

"Well, we went to that ethnic festival this spring; you know—on the Belvedere? It was really crowded and noisy, and he saved me a seat while I bought us a couple of burritos. He took a bite of his, looked it over and said, "This would really be good if it weren't for the wrap.""

Essie stuck her chin out, the way she does when she's considering something, and tilted her glance to one side. "Was there music at this festival?"

I nodded. "Lots of it, all at the same time, putting on a show, with mikes and loud-speakers; especially, loud-speakers.'

"Any young guys doing rap?"

"Yeah, you could hardly hear yourself—"

I thump my forehead and say, "Know anybody who needs an extra W?"

Essie laughs. "Looks like Greg will get his Mexican food again."

"Starting with this recipe," I assure her. "This is really good!"

Now I can talk– Drat! There's the phone again: "Hello? Oh, hi, honey! You'll never guess who came.... You're bringing who over for supper? –Just fix something simple...."

No problem. "Hey, Ty-baby. How'd you like to try that 'green-gold burritos' recipe again?"

The Monkey's Uncle
by
Leslea M. Harmon

The plane landed hard and I bounced in the nearly-comfortable seat. Its plentiful padding was bursting out of aging vinyl, as if the cushion actually had been used for a flotation device, then recycled.

"Doesn't this damned thing have shock absorbers?" The propeller was winding down loudly, and I wasn't sure if the pilot had heard, or if he'd just chosen to ignore me.

My co-passenger scratched her armpits. She stuck out a bright pink lip and picked her nose.

Nothing could be finer than to fly to Carolina…*with a monkey*.

I wasn't sure if I should scold her for her manners or strike up a conversation. I reached for my satchel on the floor, and noticed a beat-up Western discarded under the pilot's seat. *Unforgiven.* A grizzled gunslinger graced the cover. I wondered if the pilot read it while flying.

"How's our girl?" he asked, as we taxied down the airstrip for the stop. He shouted over the noise of the plane.

The orangutan or me? I wasn't sure which he meant. I glared, but decided to give him the benefit of the doubt.

"She must be someone's special pet," I said. She wore a pink floral jumper, and didn't smell too earthy—a good thing considering the temperature on this South Carolina day.

The plane slowed to a stop. A line of similar craft inched along ahead of us at the rural airport.

"I'm the monkey's uncle," he said.

"Is that right?" I asked.

He nodded, flashing a toothy grin over his shoulder.

What had Darlene gotten me into? My best friend from first grade, she'd called completely out of the blue to invite me to her wedding. Miraculously, I was able to fit it into my schedule. The whole thing was spontaneous, just Darlene's style. A great adventure, I'd thought.

All I'd known before the pilot and his "niece" arrived to retrieve me was that Darlene was marrying the man of her dreams, the reputedly tall, dark, and handsome Harold. Transportation and accommodations

were on her—she'd been delighted to provide.

She hadn't the time to talk—much to do, so little time. Just like when we were kids.

We were approaching the hanger, and I wondered what the next accommodation would bring. Perhaps the primate house in the zoo was holding a space for me.

The pilot drummed his fingers on the dash. I eyed the planes in line before us, squinting to see if I could identify any other jungle animals flying in for the wedding. Perhaps a giraffe was escorting a dashing attorney from out of town.

The props were still now, and I ventured to speak aloud without screaming.

"How long have you been flying?" I asked.

"About fifteen years. Hilda's only been flying for three."

"Her name is Hilda?" The ape had a pacifier in her mouth. "You're a team?"

He laughed. That grin again. He took off his sunglasses. Velvet-rich, chocolate-colored eyes smiled out at me.

"Yeah. She's not mine—she really does belong to my brother. I don't like to take her in the air a lot, but my brother sometimes has to leave her with me, and when I've got to work…"

"There should be affordable daycare for orangutans, right? What kind of world are we living in?" I asked.

He laughed. I liked the sound of it. Rich and deep, like his eyes. His hair was thick and dark, as well. I wondered how tall he was.

"So is your brother a big fan of *Every Which Way But Loose?*"

He turned sideways in his seat to face me. The plane was coasting now, drifting at its miniscule velocity slightly off-course.

"I know you aren't criticizing a grown man's healthy appreciation of all things Clint Eastwood."

"I didn't intend to insult—"

He laughed. "I'm just kiddin' ya. He's a primatologist." He smiled again, turning back around and righting the plane. "We're here."

Darlene and a tall, handsome man opened the plane's hatch.

"Did you enjoy the ride? Did John and Hilda treat you right?" Darlene's smile widened, her vivacious charisma entering the tiny plane though she remained on the tarmac. She held out her arms to the ape,

who scrambled into them and clutched her like a child would her mother.

The man I assumed was Harold put his hand on his brother's shoulder.

"John, why is Hilda on this plane? Did you have to put our guest through that?" He turned to greet me, and I recognized the same chocolate brown eyes and warm smile.

"I had to find out if she was a true Clint Eastwood fan, right?"

I climbed out of the plane, stretched for a moment, and shrugged. "Well, she is cute," I said.

I leaned into Darlene's shoulder and whispered. "So's her uncle."

"I'm glad you think so," she replied. "He's your date for the wedding."

Collateral Clothing

by

J. Baumgartle

One part of me is awake and knows I'm dreaming. It sees in color, but there seems to be no sound card. This adult self observes from a state of numbness, accepts that it can know but not respond.

The Felicia I have always been is at school, a beloved place, with wood floors and stairs, and large windows. The last bell has rung and my classmates are hurrying to collect the things they want to take home. –Bus drivers don't wait for you. Clocks are strictly obeyed, since parents expect their children home on schedule.

I have 'most everything–homework, band instrument and folder, half a cookie from lunch. Did I wear boots? I run to collect them, decide it would be easier to wear than carry them, set all my things down and attempt to jam them on. The halls are getting quieter and quieter. I fly down the staircase and out onto the blacktop, where a fleet of buses is building up steam for takeoff.

#3 must have parked in a different place again. I loop dangerously through the double horseshoe of gaseous yellow monsters, then realize the departure has begun. And way up near the front, already turning onto the road, is #3. My little brother and sister sway wearily in their assigned seats as they are taken out of sight.

I wake up furious, snorting air, shaking my head to rid myself of the humiliation, the too-familiar frustration–

I sleep in the next morning, which means I have to rush through routines to make it to the luncheon on time. My sister and her fiancé already have a table, by windows that overlook the park. They greet me warmly, and we all place our orders. I try to remember my sister as a little girl: the highlights in her fair hair, the refined features, a sweetness about the large blue eyes that take in everything.

The only thing that's changed about her is her depth. When Meredith speaks, her words are considered, definitive, yet kind. She and Vaughn ask me to be the matron of honor in their wedding.

–The delight of clothing itself hits me first. The blend of fabrics, the subtle language that textures speak to my fingertips, a history of

origin under the sun, all of it informed by the play of light and color as it is handled. Then, slowly, I become aware of the rare opportunity, an invitation to join in this momentous event in my sister's life. It is nearly too much. As always, I find myself virtually inundated in the swirl of sensory stimuli, to the exclusion of actual experience. I struggle to hold on, hear myself acknowledge her request, then I am in her arms, weeping, all forgotten except my very strong love for this incredible sister.

They have made plans, very detailed ones, printed them out via computer. I wonder if there is wedding software, a program with multiple choice questions, that makes you aware of all the possibilities, and upgrades or downgrades the selections according to the amount of money you are prepared to spend.

I spill my drink on my copy, but Vaughn quickly opens his lap-top and inserts cables. An outlet is behind his chair. If he had the sound on, the command he types in would go "beedle, da leep, ti-do." Doo dah. From his briefcase, a small whirring, and he lifts out another copy and hands it to me, smiling. I clasp it to me, ridiculing the relief I feel.

* * * * *

I am as nervous as I was at my own wedding. The suitcase I packed lies before me, but I'm afraid to open it for fear I've forgotten something. The bridesmaids are in the Sunday school room with me, laughing and carrying on as if they were at a party. My hair has turned out kind of funky, so I ask one of the girls for some help. She makes quick work of it, so she can get on with more interesting things.

And soon enough, I'm all by myself, hurrying to get into my dress. Wrong bra, I discover; the straps show. –Never mind, this bra converts to strapless. I take it off and remove the clasps, front and back. The white-faced clock shows twelve minutes to seven. Reassembling myself takes time, because a fingernail is breaking. The building has become strangely quiet.

The dress is the important thing. As it goes over my head, part of the hairdo comes loose, which I ignore in favor of struggling with the zipper. Whew! The music is starting. Panicked, I run to the door and find the hallway empty. Peering around the corner, I see that, far

down the hall, the wedding party has gathered. My sister beckons me. One of the ushers checks his watch.

I point to my feet, then swish, swish, swish back to the room. I almost sit on my flowers in my haste to put on the dyed shoes, stand too quickly and get one heel caught in the dress's hem. Work it loose as I hobble down the hall, bouquet stashed under one arm. The camera goes off. I glance in the gilt mirror as we enter the vestibule, and notice that I have on tangerine lipstick with my old-rose-colored dress. My escort, like the hairdresser I go to at the Radisson, deftly pulls one pin out of my hair, tucks some curls under and re-pins them with a flick of the wrist, like he's done it all his life.

The walk down the aisle seems like a gauntlet of stares to me, but then the opening fanfare of the wedding march is played and, watching my sister's poised and graceful entrance, I know I don't have to worry about another thing.

Except pictures.

Thinking Outside The Box

by

Joanna Foreman

I was strolling through the mall when a whimsical tee shirt caught my attention. If my mother were still alive, I would buy the shirt, walk over to her house next door to my own, and watch the shocked look on her face as she read the message:

If It's Not One Thing...It's Your Mother!

She would sit in her swivel rocker and think back, sorting the years, one by one, trying to figure out her failings. "Why, *Joanna*, what have I done to deserve that? I raised you the best way I knew how!"

I would have worn the shirt as a joke, so I wouldn't let her dwell on it, because, in reality, when I reminisce, I can't think of one thing my mother did wrong. Period. I say that with all the sincerity in the world. She was a fabulous mom—ask all my childhood girlfriends—they confided their jealousy, wishing their mothers were such fun, so understanding.

By now you may think this is a tale about my perfect mother. And while I did consider writing it that way, I thought better of it. When a writer concocts her mother's story, she risks losing readers if, after a paragraph or two, the narrative bogs down, gets downright boring, unless, of course, Mommy was hell on wheels. Mine was no *Mommy Dearest*. In fact, she was so ideal her story would put most people to sleep. There was one major thing she did, though, a decision she made when I was five, that altered my direction for over four decades.

There came a knock at the door, Mom answered it, and in came a group of religious zealots. They wanted to study the Bible in our home and she said yes. Just like that—her decision was made. Those people laid claim to every chair and couch cushion we owned.

"My daughter, here, has been asking questions for which I have no answers," Mom explained, "nor does my minister, it seems."

The church people nodded knowingly, as if to indicate they alone could satisfy my mother's need for resolution. Now I have no idea what question a five-year-old could ask for which a response would be so difficult, but I suppose it was probably one of those meaning-of-life inquiries little kids have at one time or another. Perhaps I had asked, "Why am I here?" and it had freaked her out. I don't think she knew why *she* was here, so how could that be remedied? Mom hoped to find meaningful solutions in this home Bible class, which eventually lasted nearly three years, after which she joined the religion whole-hog, with me following up the rear. Dad stood silently at the sidelines and watched.

At first, I thought it was really neat the way I didn't have to ponder issues for myself anymore. It seemed such a relief—the church had a ready-made answer for each and every question that popped into my little head. So cool—I could spend all of my days thinking of dolls and toys, and, through the years, clothes, homework, and...boys! Nothing any heavier than that. What a load off that was.

But, just once I had to ask: "How could we possibly know for sure Jesus was born on December 25th?"

Oops, turns out he wasn't. "Everyone knows that," the religion's spokesperson said. "Check out a Catholic encyclopedia. It will have an accurate and thorough history of the holiday and its origin."

Mom investigated right away. She said, since it wasn't really the day of Christ's birth, we would stop celebrating Christmas. What a bummer! I loved the scent of a fresh evergreen tree in the living room, aglow with bubble lights, strings of popcorn and tinsel, the train running around in a circle underneath surrounded by presents! And get this: December 25 was my dad's birthday, but he simply lit a Camel, popped the top off another Schlitz, and said, "*Christ-My-Ass,* it's all about commercialism anyway." He'd said this about Christmas for years, so his indifference to Mom's refusal to celebrate came as no surprise. His parents, brother and sisters took it in stride, shaking their heads while murmuring polite, whispered questions they didn't know I overheard: *What has she gotten herself into? Do you think maybe it's a phase she's going through?*

Then, all of a sudden, we didn't celebrate birthdays at all, not even *mine*! Something about John the Baptist's head being chopped

off at a pagan birthday party, and, at a prostitute's request, served on a silver platter. We wouldn't want to be associated with such merrymaking, now would we? Well, *I* still felt special on my birthday, but I wasn't allowed to have my neighborhood friends in for a party. No cake, no presents. I wrote *Happy Birthday, Joanna* in my diary each year on October 5th.

Apparently, when Jesus had instructed his followers to celebrate his death he failed to mention his birth or resurrection, thus Easter was out. Each year around Easter time we'd congregate and listen to a sermon about Jesus' death, then pass wine and bread around, symbols of his sacred flesh and blood, but no one partook of anything. If Dad had gone along with us, he would have said, "What a waste of good booze."

It pained me to lose the Easter Bunny. I had delighted in searching for my pretty basket overfilled with colorfully dyed eggs and chocolate rabbits. Mom always hid it in the same place, behind the drapes at our living-room window. It was obvious the way one curtain stuck out farther than the others, but I pretended to search all over the house before I looked there, with Mom following me everywhere I went, excited to watch me find the treasure she had so lovingly prepared.

Fourth of July came along and, lo and behold, it got nixed, too. People in our religion didn't celebrate national holidays, nor were they patriotic in any way. They didn't vote, salute the flag or stand for the National Anthem. *Neutrality* was a word I heard quite often from the pulpit. You can imagine the grief that caused me in school. My schoolmates were unmerciful in the '50's, called me a traitor and the dirtiest word of all—a Communist!

Guess what happened next: The Devil's Holiday, Halloween. Yep, no longer up for grabs. No more fun and scary costumes—no more candy. My neighborhood pals would share a modest amount of their booty with me on November 1st, but mostly they gave me their apples and raisins. Gee, thanks, I'd think sarcastically. "Never look a gift horse in the mouth," Mom would say. I'd roll my eyes and put the fruit into a bowl on our kitchen table. No, thank you. I had had pure, unadulterated chocolate in mind.

Thanksgiving rolled around, and we had a family dinner every

year with all of my aunts, uncles and cousins. My mother superbly roasted a turkey stuffed with sage and celery dressing. She whipped up creamy mashed potatoes, smooth homemade gravy, and cranberry sauce made from fresh berries. She candied yams with marshmallow topping, baked hot yeast rolls and velvety pumpkin pies. I helped her set our table with a linen cloth, china, crystal and real silverware.

The confusion for me was that our religion prescribed Thanksgiving Day should be no different than any other, we would be just as thankful the other 364 days of the year; one day should not be set aside from another. Yet, we didn't have meals like *that* just any other day. My mouth waters at the very memory of it. Thanksgiving Day was special, and while I felt hypocritical, I didn't say it aloud, for the next year I might have gotten a bologna sandwich, something I wasn't willing to risk.

I grew up in Indianapolis on Stratford Avenue in a small, cape-cod style house. All my friends on our street had the identical house, although some were turned the opposite direction from mine. Kids learn their social skills from one another, and mostly from children in their school or neighborhood. To have a close-knit peer group you need some things in common. Now you can do the math: I never went to birthday parties or threw one of my own. I no longer had a Christmas tree. I didn't exchange Valentine cards, or even join in with the kids on my block waving sparklers in their front yards at dusk on the Fourth of July. I had no Easter dress to show off in the spring, and no frilly princess costume for show-and-tell on October 31st. One Halloween, the first and second graders were paraded through the school's hallways, which were lined with older students. Of course, I was the little girl at the end of the line without a costume, and the responses from one out of ten big kids were these: "Look at that ugly little witch. Oh, she's scary looking. What a freak!" Need I say more?

As a teenager, I became distant from my childhood friends, or maybe they withdrew from me. As far as the religion went, that was exactly the way it was supposed to be. We were discouraged from associating with worldly people. Anyone who wasn't in our religion was considered worldly, a distraction from pure worship.

"We're doing things God's way, the Christian way," my mother said, "and our reward will come in the future when we live forever in Paradise. So be a good girl and be patient...after all, Jesus was persecuted, too." I wondered why, if Jesus had been mistreated and died for me, did I

have to go through similar harassment?

I saw the television advertising in the '60's for my Dad's favorite beer: "You only go around once in life, so you have to grab for all the gusto you can get!" Gusto, how I loved that word. I figured it was probably a sin, but I wanted my gusto *now*. The future seemed such a long time off for the reward Mom said Christians were promised.

My future finally arrived in 1997 when I was fifty years old. It was something somebody said, my trust was blatantly betrayed, and I put one foot in front of the other and walked out of the box I'd been hiding in for forty-five years. Ironically, my mother had died eighteen months before. Had I waited all that time so I wouldn't disappoint her? Perhaps.

Undoubtedly the *old school* way of thinking for a number of people was this: if my parents' religion was good enough for them, then it was good enough. However, I am a baby-boomer, which gives me license to think for myself.

After all of those years, thinking for myself was daunting at first. When I say I walked out of the box, I do so with all due respect to religion. Some religion's boundaries are so strict that the space is as confining as the one I've already described, while other religions give their followers such leeway, the box could better be described as an overseas shipping container. I believe everyone should have the right to choose whether they want to be in a box, a religion, or not. Some people peek out of the lid from time to time, crawl partially out, but never leave, simply sit on the edge, and are usually miserable with their indifference. Others, labeled as evil sinners, have been literally thrown out of their religion, and more often than not their behavior heads rapidly in a downward spiral from vaguely spiritual to out-of-control. I've known a handful of both kinds of people.

In my case, since I simply walked away, my behavior didn't disintegrate, nor was I miserable since I was positive about my choice from the beginning. But it was a quantum leap, and I was frustrated for nearly two years and didn't know where to turn. Frustration and confusion because I had left behind a church which I had trusted, one in which I had felt safe, and moved into an area where I had to make my own rules for once in my life. It had been ingrained in me that the religion I was in was the one and only, so where did I stand with God now that I

was no longer a part of it?

I headed straight for the self-help department of my local bookstore, something I had been discouraged from doing all those years. I read many books, *The Power of Now,* and *Conversations With God,* being two of my favorites. I attended a scattering of New Age meetings, and one beautiful day I found my paradise when I turned one room of my home into what I called The Meditation Room. My grown sons teased me when they dubbed it The Medication Room. I was finally searching for answers myself, something I could have done a long time ago if I had made that choice. I had always been taught I had to look outside myself, heavenward, for God. How delighted I was to discover my answers within! The tools I used were my heart, my conscience and my common sense. After all, weren't those God-given gifts, the heart, conscience and common sense? If we weren't meant to use them, why else would they have been given to us?

On my road to spirituality, religion had become an obstacle, so I maneuvered around and away from it. I am where I'm supposed to be. I share holidays now with that gusto I always wanted—with my family: my husband, sons and grandchildren.

My view of the entire human race has changed since I'm no longer in a "cult" that puts itself above and separate from it. I have left guilt behind and have lost the fear of displeasing God.

A childhood friend who remains a staunch member of the church was on the phone, shocked to hear the news that I had followed a different path. When she anxiously asked, "What about the future?" I was stunned for a moment—I had forgotten how important the future was to those people. I'm sure my response, "Oh, not to worry. It will get here someday, but I'm enjoying the present moment too much to concern myself with it," convinced her that I had become a heathen for sure—no everlasting life in paradise for me. I wanted to say, "Chill out, girl," but it would have been pointless. None of my friends from the *church era* keep in touch—we have nothing in common anymore.

Mom spent a lot of time in her kitchen, as most housewives did in the '50's and '60's. She taught me her recipe for a magnificent pie crust—just the right amount of shortening, flour, salt and ice water; mix well and roll it out into a circle. Lay it gently in a pie plate, fill it up with something delectable, and bake. What ultimate satisfaction when the pie

comes out of the oven and you see and taste the results of your efforts!

I'm that pie who turned out okay after all. My mother watches over me, happy to see me thriving in my own way. I finally realize that's what she wanted all along.

Throw Momma From the Dive Boat
by
Ginny Fleming

The diving advertisements enticed, the colors of the new scuba gear seduced, and my husband's offer of vacations to sultry waters was one I couldn't refuse. So, I signed up for scuba class. You may well ask why a much stressed and frazzled woman would take a dive class. Simply put, I did it for love. Love of diver-husband and love of exotic white-sand beaches. But, contrary to what the Beatles taught us, LOVE is not all you need.

First, you need good thorough training with a fully-qualified safety-minded scuba instructor. Second, purchase your basic equipment: mask, fins, snorkel, gloves. A small water-proof slate inscribed in indelible, not to mention waterproof, ink with the assuring words 'DON'T PANIC!!' written in 3" block letters is also *very* helpful. The training came from a local dive shop. I had to make my own sign.

Classes began with book instruction. The instructor, "Mark the Shark", informed us about all the things that *could* happen while scuba diving, and all the things that *wouldn't* happen while scuba diving. The coulds greatly outweighed the wouldn'ts. I quickly caressed my waterproof sign. I looked back to Mark. He was regaling us with the old chestnut: "There are old divers and there are bold divers, but there aren't any old bold divers." He ended this quote with insane cackling.

We studied equipment and reviewed more possible hazards to uncareful divers. It occurred to me, the first couple of classes were to weed out the faint-hearted and weak-kneed. I wondered aloud, like an idiot, what class would take care of the fools like me who go where angels fear to tread. Mark hung his head and muttered, "There's always one in every class...."

The next class arrived and Mark quickly put me at ease with the equipment. By the end of the session, he'd convinced me land-walkers could actually breathe through a regulator, and I released my death grip on the side of the pool. I have to admit, I honestly *did* enjoy diving through the warm water.

After executing (forget I used that word) a practiced assent, I broke the surface, spat out the regulator and crowed, "This is like flying

without the airplane! And I didn't even have to go through the metal detector!"

Mark hung his head and muttered, "A wasted mind is a terrible thing...."

My student trip was in Florida with the manic and highly skilled diving instructor, along with the surviv... ehhhh... *remaining* students. First stop: a springs a gorgeously-beautiful, off-road finger-shoot of the Everglades (*Everglades???* Hey! Wait just a dang minute... *What keeps the alligators out?* ...forget I brought that up...) where the water is a constant temperature and the mosquitoes whistle *Dixie* while tugging at the zippers of your wetsuit.

We walked backward into the crystal-clear water, my web-footed footsteps accompanied by a gleeful death-dirge in my mind, and slowly descended about fifteen feet, where I noticed a slight trouble with the pressure in my ears they wouldn't clear. Very few new divers have troubles with their ears, but mine were caused from a silly little failure to blow air out through my nose.

The Shark frantically flashed underwater hand signals, some of which I strongly believe to be obscene. I tried and tried to blow air through my nose, but to no avail. Finally in desperation, I thought of my husband waiting for me back home.

The picture of my loving spouse appeared in my troubled mind and I heard his musical voice in my unequalized ears: *"Dear? Mind if I pop down to the Bahamas for some diving with the guys and leave you at home?"* I blew air out through my nose. My ears opened up (or so I thought) and Mark quickly took credit for another wimp-diver saved.

We continued down to a depth of fifty feet to the wide entrance of a small cavern, about the size of my kitchen. The spacious opening was as large as the little room I left back home. I could have put a nice-sized stove in the corner... a small side-by-side to the left of that... topped off with a lovely set of carved-oak cabinets and a sweet faux-marble countertop Oh! And don't forget a mini-bar for entertaining. So, instead of a large cavern, it was more a "Nook and Cranny Formation". I believe that's the highly technical scientific terminology used in the diving community.

Feeling a grave (poor choice of words...) reluctance to enter much like the feeling I have about my own kitchen, I hesitated. But

Mark gave me his spare flashlight (*Jeez-O-Pete* he's not flirting with me *is he???*) and I noticed the other students were going in and for the most part coming out, so in a moment of desperate insanity I thought: Why not?

Entering the mouth of the cavern with Mark, I noticed it was dark, dingy and very quiet in the dim-lit little room. The other students were mesmerized, sitting very still. My wild-eyed Diving-Guru (*another* highly technical diving term) motioned for me to ascend to an underwater air pocket for an intimate and informative talk.

"Did you see the eels?" he burbled. "*And-And-And* did you see the one swimming directly at *Darlene?*"

"Eels?" I queried, composed and frantically grabbing Mark's comforting arm, "*EELS?!?* You mean I'm fifty feet underwater in a dark cave and there are *EELS* swimming around me?" I longed for my waterproof sign, but alas, I'd left it on land in the trunk of the car.

To be truthful, the swim back to the surface was really pleasant and beautiful, what I could see of it, and I vowed to get prescription lenses installed in my mask when I returned home. Side note: For a little understanding of my visual experience in the lovely and picturesque spring, coat your eyeballs with petroleum jelly. On second thought don't. I *really* don't need the lawsuits.

My next dive was the following day, six miles off shore in the Gulf. The boat ride out was a lot of fun. The early morning fog made it impossible to see ten feet from the bow, and some silly idiot *me* had chosen a seat beside the noxious fume-spewing engine. Then the captain shut down the boat's motors and stomachs started to roll. I didn't realize stomachs could roll in so many different directions at once. Mark was already over the side, calling my name, adding gleefully: "Come on in, it's a good day to dive!"

What with the wave's sickly slap on the side of the boat, I could have sworn he said: 'Die'.

I gamely made my way to the deck's railing, and called down to Mark: "I feel sick."

"What?"

"I don't think I should dive today. I really do feel queasy."

"That's no excuse. You're just a wimp diver," he grinned. "Besides, that little sea-sickness will go away when you get down

under the water."

It's really hard to see the glint in the eye of a pathological liar wearing a dive mask. You see, the sea-sickness *does* pass away (forget I said *pass away*) when you get down but first you've got to *get down*.

I made my giant stride, a carefully choreographed step off the boat into the sea (or in my case, a weak-stomach-rolling-in-opposition-to-the-boat *leap*) and landed in the water with my mask rearranged on my face. Forthwith, I took control of the situation and hyperventilated.

Mark laughed maniacally in sympathy and concern, leading me to the guide rope. But, when I gripped the hemp-braided Holy Grail, to keep us from being separated in the bobbing waves, he suddenly changed his mind and frantically requested me to release the rope.

The exchange went something like this:

MARK
"Let go of the rope."
ME
"No, I'd rather not, if you don't mind."
MARK
"Let go of the rope."
ME
"If it's all the same to you, I don't believe I will. I found
it, nobody else is using it at the moment, and it's my
last link to the surface world and life as I know it."
MARK
"Let *GO* of the rope!!"
ME
"Is it that important to you? Fine. So be it.
I'll just drift off out into the foggy ocean and
never be seen again. That's all right, don't
let it concern you. I've lived a full life."
MARK
"I *said* LET GO OF THE *FR#$*&@K*ing* ROPE!!!"

I found out later I had hold of Mark's index finger and had managed to crush calcium deposits it'd taken years to build up in his joints. If

he'd only taken the time to calmly explain the situation, I'd have let go of his finger I merely wanted the rope! Sheesh! *Men!*

When my equilibrium returned and I could breath again, we descended without incident. There were colorful denizens of the deep, such as "Finding Nemo" clownfish, genteel-mannered damselfish, majestic Queen Angels, coral-eating parrotfish, slowly skittering sea urchins, antennae-waving lobsters, privacy-loving moray eels, ingeniously-camouflaging octopi, vegetarian nurse sharks (just kidding checking to see if you were paying attention), I wish I could say I *saw* these wondrous sights, but I didn't. If you've been paying attention (and if not, *LISTEN UP* why don't'cha or I'll break out the petroleum jelly) you'll remember my vision problems. I was for all intents and purposes *BLIND!*

The only thing I could make out was Mark, and at eighty feet he surely was a beautiful sight. Amazing how when you're at the bottom of the ocean with a strange man (and man, was Mark strange), he suddenly turns into Brad Pitt.

We returned to the surface and I immediately recognized the queasiness again. I'd barely removed my gear when I discovered a great desire to rush to the side of the boat, and it wasn't because I wanted to wave to the other divers. Convincing my instructor I was done diving for the day, I clung to the wall of the boat cabin for support and comfort until the captain decided to fire up the engines for the ride back to the bay. Magically, my stomach settled down! In the future, I'm searching for a captain who allows giant strides at full speed ahead.

I returned home exhausted and uncertified, as Mark rightly felt I should be calmer in the water before he'd sign my card. We agreed I'd make more open-water dives and he'd retain the further motion of his finger joint. It was a fair agreement, settled to our mutual satisfaction.

Mysteriously, a tiny clue surfaced (clever how I used *that* word, right?) after I'd returned home. A doctor's visit revealed, while in the bucolic, eel-laden spring, my little problem with blowing air out my nose had resulted in a matching pair of ruptured eardrums. *Ah-Ha!*, says I, *Mayhaps THAT'S why equilibrium remained just out of reach while I clung to the Heaven-sent dive rope. Mayhaps Just mayhaps, mind you, if after healing, that is IF I were to return to the dive boat*

with Mark... Oh, get real. Mayhaps pigs will fly.

I've since made my dives, gotten calmer in the water and received my card, though Mark refuses to shake my hand and he's not jumping at the chance to dive with me. His reluctance *is* a puzzlement.

Would I do it all over again? Yes. Would I do it differently? Does the Pope swim? I really don't know the answer to this one, and I've asked every Catholic I can find (Strangely, they silently make the sign of the cross, mournfully shake their head, and quickly walk away... What? *What???* Was it something I said?).

And as for Mark the Shark's theory of there not being any old bold divers: I may never be a bold diver, but I fully intend to be an old diver. I'm looking forward to future nursing home dive-trips. I've heard those old codgers can really get down!

Wild Garden Mixture
by
J. Baumgartle

Every year of my childhood
I bought a packet of
"Wild Garden Mixture,"
caught again by the picture
on the front, a fantasy
of variety and color
just waiting to come to life.
I can still feel
the paper in my hands,
the vellum smoothness
of the greeting card illustration.
We already had woods flowers,
the color like nothing else
you could experience:
translucent blues,
eager yellows,
pink-tinged whites.
More beauty
could only be better.
Wild flowers grow between
tree roots, of course,
so that's where
the tiny seeds were scattered,
under the old oak tree
on the hillside.

Every year I waited
for shoots to appear,
sporadically checked the ground
which remained as hard as
concrete.
My family began to tease me
about it–Oh, yes,
Jeannine's "Wild Garden
Mixture"
–since I never learned my
lesson.
Over time I realized
plants need more than love.
I had to understand their needs,
respect their nature,
not just toss them at God's feet
with instructions.
Perhaps "wild" and "garden"
growths were incompatible,
one an opportunist, one
cultivated.
I wanted the best of both worlds,
exuberance and docility,
untouched freshness,
and picking rights.

Contributors

The Southern Indiana Writers Group has been more-or-less together since 1992. We began meeting monthly in a conference room in a local hospital. We now meet weekly to exchange information and expertise on everything from computers to poetry. The group also serves as a critique forum (in the same sense that a pack of wolves serves as food critics). Membership is limited, but visitors are welcome, and have been known to fit in so well they become members against their better judgment.

Bonnie Abraham After twenty-five plus years of writing letters disqualifying people from Unemployment Benefits, she retired in order to write something more pleasant. She writes short stories (many with Biblical themes), poetry and devotionals. Currently, she resides in Corydon with her mother's ghost.

Marian Allen lives in a big house in a little wood, which is not the only difference between Allen and Laura Ingels Wilder. Allen has three novels on electronic disk (alternatively known as "coasters"). She has published stories in print and on-line magazines, including Marion Zimmer Bradley's FANTASY Magazine, The Phone Book, PanGaia and Oceans of the Mind.

Jeannine Baumgartle writes poetry and fiction. Her work has appeared in publications such as *Green Meadow Press, Flying Island, Literally,* and Studio: *A Journal for Christians Writing* and won a residency for poetry at the Mary Anderson Center for the Arts . She and her husband live in the small town of Crandall.

Ginny Fleming considers herself to be foremost a screenwriter, as this is her favorite media. Because nobody thought to tell her she couldn't, after optioning 3 scripts for the unsold ensemble sitcom *"Tia"* (any producers reading this?), Fleming dived head-first into the shark-infested mulligan stew (How's that for mixing metaphors?) that is Hollywood scriptwriting. Her romantic comedy scripts can be previewed at *The Spec Script Library, Writer's Market,* and *Writers.Net.*

Fleming's take on hysterical fantasy (funny, that is), a novel she likes to call *Dragonsayver* (when she's not calling it Melvin), is a "Shrek-like" novel just begging to be made into an animated film (Fleming wonders if she should shove a tin cup in its hand and drop it on a busy intersection....). Besides her annual contribution to SIW anthology and a brief appearance in the Louisville Courier Journal, Fleming is busy finding a home for *Keys of Illusion*, a Romantic/Suspense novel filled with magic, scuba, fantasy, a bunch of lavender stuff and little bit of sex. Multiple scripts are always in the works whenever Fleming manages to "channel" Jimmy Buffett, her "Muse" (Yeah, she knows Jimmy's not dead -- Hopes for his continued good health, in fact -- That just makes him easier to channel).

Joanna Foreman has one main claim to fame: She has successfully raised three sons and has two grandchildren who are still too young to be anything less than perfect. She writes short fiction and slice-of-life vignettes, and recently published her first collection of short stories: Ghosts of Interstate 65. She and her husband, Craig, married barefooted on St. Augustine Beach in 2001. They built a modest home in the middle of two wooded acres in Georgetown, Indiana, where they will happily ever after. Visit Joanna at www.joannaforeman.com

L. M. Harmon is a freelance writer and newspaper columnist in New Albany, Indiana. Her column on family life, Guerilla Mothering, can be read in the New Albany Tribune and Jeffersonville Evening News, and select newspapers in the Community Holdings network of publications. Additionally, she is the host and creator of Allergy News - All the News That Itches, and writes commercially for fun and profit. Her first novel, This Brilliant Darkness, was completed in 2005 and then re-completed several times after that, until finally pronounced "ready" in the fall of 2007. She is currently writing a non-fiction self-help book on the topic of Food Allergies, about which she wishes she knew nothing, but unfortunately knows quite a lot. In order to join Southern Indiana Writers, she was required to milk a wild boar and kidnap a man, so if you don't like her work, do not mention it.

T Lee Harris is a writer and illustrator who has been a lover of mystery and the detective genre since discovering books. A graduate of Indiana University with a Bachelor of Fine Arts, T has been involved with radio production, game design, comic books and desktop publishing. Interests include participation in the Society for Creative Anachronism and Renaissance Faires, tailoring authentic costuming for re-enactors and playing online roleplaying games. Several novels are in progress featuring Sitehuti and Nefer-Djenou-Bastet, Josh Katzen and a series set in ninth century Ireland.

Jane E. Jones truly has her head in the clouds. (She lives so high on a hill she can see the Tunder-Over-louisville fireworks from 40 miles away.) She's been a legal secretary for twenty-plus years and uses writing to escape from the long-winded legalese she deals with daily. She writes romantic adventures and paranormal fiction and is currently working on the final installment of a three-novel series.

Joy Kirchgessner is a business woman, illustrator and writer. Her Paintings were recently on tour with the Kentucky National Art and Wildlife Exhibition. She shares her home with her husband and two horses.

Glenda Mills resides with her husband, three children, and the mortal remains of four dogs, a cat, various hamsters, turtles, frogs and fish in Floyd County, IN. When she is not busy being a "stay-at-home" mom, which is seldom, she enjoys writing poetry, non-fiction and fiction. Her work crosses genres and presently includes short stories, poems, a finished manuscript on an introspective look at the miscarriage of her child, and an unfinished manuscript of a "slightly" psychotic female serial killer. She firmly belives that variety is the spice of life.

Teddi Robinson has taken several creative writing classes and has (With a lot of encouragement) just published her first book, *The Meddlers*. She is currently at work polishing the sequel for publication before the end of 2008.

Previous Publications by
Southern Indiana Writers

Indian Creek Anthology
Ghost Writers
Christmas Bizarre
Dragon: Our Tales
Grounds for Suspicion
2000 Tales
Way Out West
Unbridled Lust
There's Something Under the Bedtime Stories
Novel Ingredients
Write of Passage
Off the Rack
Beastly Tales

Coming in 2008

Most Wanted

Visit our web site for excerpts of previous publications
and availability information:

http://siw.artisanpath.com

www.ingramcontent.com/pod-product-compliance
Lightning Source LLC
Chambersburg PA
CBHW031854170626
46807CB00004B/1716

* 9 780615 184951 *